The Great
Tejon Club
Jubilee

The Great Tejon Club Jubilee

Stories by Gerald W. Haslam

Illustrations by Don Mahan

DEVIL MOUNTAIN BOOKS
WALNUT CREEK, CALIFORNIA

Gerald W. Haslam

The Great Tejon Club Jubilee

DEVIL MOUNTAIN BOOKS, P.O. BOX 4115,
WALNUT CREEK, CA 94596. ALL RIGHTS RESERVED.

Editorial assistant: Barbara Sturges

Cover design: Wayne Gallup

Cover illustration: Don Mahan

Typesetter: Encore Design & Type, Martinez, CA

Typestyle: Palatino

Library of Congress Cataloging-in-Publication Data

Haslam, Gerald W.
    The Great Tejon Club Jubilee: Stories by Gerald W. Haslam; illustrations by Don Mahan.
    p. cm.
    ISBN 0-915685-09-4
    1. Central Valley (Calif.: Valley)—Social life and customs—fiction. 2. Bars (Drinking establishments)—California—Central Valley (Valley)—Fiction. 3. Community life—California—Central Valley (Valley)—Fiction. 4. Working class—California—Central Valley (Valley)—Fiction. 5. Men—California—Central Valley (Valley)—Fiction.
    I. Title.
    PS3558.A724G74 1996
    813'.54—dc20   95-16037
[B]   CIP

23•9876

For Justin Meyer, Dick Kirpatrick,
Jim Lee, Max Westbrook, Jim Hill,
Duke Dominguez, Terry Alexander,
Glen Love, Jim Houston,
and, of course, Sam Clemens...
chismosos extraordinarios!

CONTENTS

PREFACE

There is a Tejon Club. It is the neighborhood tavern where my dad and his friends gathered in Oildale, half a block up the street from our house, half a block down the street from Buck Owens' Enterprises. It's also where Billy Thorp and Jimmy Thomas and Merle Haggard and I learned to shoot pool nearly fifty years ago.

There is no Bob Don Bundy or Big Dunc or Earl, no Shoat Wilhite or Wylie Hillis or Jerry Bill Hogsett. They are figments of my imagination, in no way based on the actual people who assemble or have assembled at the Tejon Club.

Their antics *are*, however, based on something I learned at the tavern when I was young: the rough camaraderie of working men. It was a male domain in those years, seldom visited by women. Devilment, contentiousness, kidding, and the bursting of illusions were common activities. The tall-tale tradition was alive and well, as was just plain bullshit.

One afternoon, for instance, a young roughneck brought a new girlfriend into the club for a beer. "He was just showing her off," my father explained. As the couple departed, one of the boys called out, "Hey, Richard, I forgot to congratulate you on gettin' that case of clap cleared up." The maiden was blinking, and Richard was glowering, as he hustled her out the door.

The tone of the place was populist in the old sense. Most of the patrons were union men. Big shots, in general, were regarded with suspicion, as were the national currents of social change that seemed to be accelerating. Most of the men were old-line Democrats who discovered to their surprise that they were becoming Republicans as their political party drifted left. In 1972, one said to me

ix

with genuine amazement, "I had to vote for that damn *Nixon!*"

The Tejon Club really was more like a club than a saloon. Those rough-hewn men cared about one another and about one another's kin. They were also generous, quick to take up a collection for any reasonable cause. Most of them had survived the Great Depression, and they regarded work as something sacred. A pauper of any color seeking employment would always find something at the club. A good worker — no matter what the job — was greatly respected: "Ol' Jim Bob'll do to take along, by God." And a lousy one was scorned: "That Darryl ain't worth a can a cold piss."

Most of the men had been raised in the border South — Texas, Arkansas, Louisiana, Missouri — in an earlier time. As a result, I occasionally heard bursts of racist rhetoric at the club, but I also saw that ancient prejudice ignored in the face of pragmatic reality: A Mexican or black who was a good worker was also eligible to be considered a good guy, the highest compliment I ever heard employed there, though in truth standards seemed to me to be set higher for nonwhites.

Given the realities of their time and place, those men were reasonable models. And I guess that remains the bottom line for me. Although my dad and most of his cronies are now dead, I'm delighted they had the club, and that I did too. It was our neighborhood's male gathering spot, its sweat house. I hope that, at some eternal bar in the sky, Pop and Elmer and Al and Tom and Monty and the rest are still laughing and joshing, kidding a pompous foreman, and that they consider these stories they inspired to be acceptable work.

Most of all, I hope they think I've grown up to be a good guy.

Speck Haslam's son, Gerry

The Great Tejon Club Jubilee

Stories by Gerald W. Haslam

Illustrations by Don Mahan

The Great Disclaimer!!!

Do Not Never Read More'n One Of These
Bullshit Deals At A Time, And Also Read
'Em In Order Too.

Okay, that's what my wife Heddy, that she's a school teacher and a prune-picker to boot, she told me to tell you folks...or somethin' like that anyways. She said put one of them Surgeon-General deals on the book like what's on cigarette packs, and I don't smoke no more.

"How come one of them deals?" I asked her.

She said, "It wouldn't be good for you if people read them out of sequence or to read more than one at a sitting."

"For *me?* Don't you mean it wouldn't be good for *them?*"

"No, I mean *you.* Somebody might throttle you."

"Oh yeah! Well, somebody might get their ass kicked, too!" I snapped right back, then I seen she was a-grinnin', just joshin' me I believe. That got me to laughin' myownself. She's a good ol' gal, Heddy.

1

Anyways, I never exactly *wrote* these deals. I just told 'em to Speck Haslam's pencil-neck kid, that Gerald that he couldn't play football worth a bent nail. And he ain't no kid no more, neither, about as old as Noah's goat. So if you want to kick somebody's ass, kick his.

You get hold of me, pardner, and won't nobody have to tell you to turn a-loose! Bet your sweet nickel on that.

Yours truly,
Jerry Bill Hogsett
Semi-Author

The Great Kern County Gator Hunt

You shoulda heard the boys roar whenever ol' Wylie Hillis he busted into the Tejon Club that evenin' just a-frothin' at the mouth. Us guys we liked to fell off our bar stools. We think ol' Wylie's funny from the git-go. I mean he not only believes some of the damndest things, but everywhere he goes he wears these baggy old work coveralls that zip up the front like he wore in the oilfields before he retired. He's a stylish sucker. I think he sleeps in them damn things.

"I see you're wearin' your tuxedo today," I right away said when he come in. Us guys we like to hard-ass him a little about that outfit, and whenever he showed up lookin' so agitated we just figgered on givin' him a rough time like always, but he never said nothin' about his clothes.

"Oh Lord!" he gasped. "Guess what I seen right smack in the Kern River where I'uz fishin'." He stopped to catch his breath, then said, "A gi'nt gator!"

3

"Beertender," I hollered at Earl that owns the joint, "gimme some a what ol' Wylie's been a-drinkin' 'cause it's sure worked good on him." That give the boys a kick.

"Yer ass, Jerry Bill!" was all the ol' Arkie said, and I have to admit he did look scared, his eyes all bugged out. He's about half-faintified anyways, if you was to ask me — weaker'n a popcorn fart.

"Sheee-it, Wylie," sang out Big Dunc that worked on the county road crew, "you sure it wadn't no lizard out for a swim, see?" Dunc he was hunched over a beer, his jeans a-droopin' in back as per usual on account of the butt-fairy havin' flew right past him whenever he'uz a baby. That's okay, though, 'cause the gut-fairy blessed him at least twice. Anyways, about a foot of his moon was a-grinnin' at us, and we'd give serious consideration to takin' up a collection to buy him some suspenders...or a butt transplant. He's about half-stylish hisownself.

"Damnit, Duncan, I spent me a lotta time workin' in East Texas and Lou'siana, so I damn sure know a gator whenever I see one," the old man snapped.

Bob Don Bundy, that graduated Bakersfield Junior College, he kinda laughed. "Heck, Wylie, gators are warm water animals. That Kern River'd freeze a gator's nuts off." He's a smart sucker, Bob Don. That's how come he works in a office.

You'd think that information from a educated man would of stopped Wylie Hillis, but no. "Then there's a nutless gator cruisin' over yonder, *Perfesssor*," he sorta spit that last word.

Earl that was wipin' a beer glass, and rollin' that toothpick around his mouth like always, he said to Larry, the relief bartender, "Well, he oughta be mean, what with his nut problem and all."

"You go fartin' around the Kern River, Earl," warned the Arkie, "and you might just have a little nut problem of yer own."

"Hell," I said real fast, "ol' Earl's always had a *little* nut problem. Just ask his ol' lady."

"Ask *your* ol' lady!" barked the proprietor while everybody but cept Wylie was laughin'.

Well Earl he served Wylie a beer while the rest of us we was waitin' on the ol' poop to calm down a tad so's we could figger out what he really *had* seen. But Wylie he stuck to his guns, swearin' up and down he'd saw a gator. When we told him wasn't no way a gator could live in that cold water, he just shrugged, "Go tell that to the gator."

We'd been pullin' purty good on tonsil varnish all afternoon, it bein' a ballgame Saturday and all, and we always ragged ol' Wylie purty good, so Bob Don he right away suggested we might could drive out there and check on the misplaced gator, winkin' at me and grinnin'. I caught right on; "Why not?" I agreed.

Wylie he took the bait, jumpin' off his stool. "Come own, boys," he barked. "I'll run ye out there myownself."

"Why not?" I said again.

We all piled into the ol' Arkie's pickup, him and Big Dunc fillin' the cab while me and Earl and Bob Don we worked on fresh beers in the back. Out we bounded past Standard School, beyond the Golden Bear oil refinery, and onto a service road where we used to go rabbit huntin' when we was kids, then off on a dirt track, dust boilin' up behind us as we headed toward them high bluffs above the river.

Ever since they built that dam up in Isabella in the fifties back when I was just a hard-peckered kid, we ain't got much water down here most years. But this was a real wet one, so it was almost like ol' times, with the Kern River even overflowin' into some side channels that'd been dry for a long spell. Maybe it was seein' all that water or maybe the long, warm, kinda orange-blue evenin' we get in Kern County, but I never felt so cocky whenever Wylie he finally stopped his truck. *Sheee-it,* that place it looked flat spooky to me.

5

To make matters worse, ol' Wylie'd been after cat-fish way to hell and gone in the big middle of it, so we had to walk about a damn mile, it gettin' darker and darker, animal sounds all around us: bullfrogs startin', then a coyote singin' real lonesome, then half the dogs in Oildale givin' him hell, and even some birds screechin'. Then come a roar couldn't none of us identify, half like a diesel horn, half like a horny cow — hell of a noise.

"Wh-wh-what's that dang thing?" stuttered Bob Don, not soundin' all that confident no more.

"A bull gator," proclaimed ol' Wylie with this I-told-ya-so tone in his voice.

"Bullshit!" I snapped, my own voice louder than I expected 'cause I was a little edgy. "Ain't no damn gators in California."

Ol' Wylie he wouldn't budge: "That's a gator for damn sure."

"No way," said Earl. I believe he'd swallowed that toothpick.

"Hah!" snorted Wylie. The ol' poop he was gettin' cocky out there in the damn wilderness. Hell, we must of been a good five miles from town. Anyways, he commenced walkin' deeper and deeper into it, us guys followin' but not too happy about it. To make matters worse, the moon it went behind the only damn cloud in Kern County, and everythin' turned even darker.

"He-he!" cackled Bob Don and I knew he was scared shitless.

We finally reached this little channel that was part of the river's overflow from last year whenever it'd went and rained to beat hell. I'd gigged frogs there once or twice over the years. Big Dunc, that'd been silent as a turd, he spoke right up: "No gators here, see. Let's go."

"Hell," chuckled Wylie, "I never said the gator was right here. It's in the river yonder." He snapped on the big flashlight he was carryin' and said, "Lemme show you boys how we usta hunt gators back in Lou'siana." He sent the beam across that frog pond. "You gotta look for the reflection of their eyes, little red mean deals," he lectured.

Behind us some kind of animal it busted through the bushes, and I liked to lost my beer right there. Me, to tell the truth, I really wished I was somewheres else...*anywheres* else. Bob Don he taken off after he heard that but stopped real quick. He couldn't remember which way to go in that dark. "Oh *heck!*" he said; whenever he got that close to cussin', you knew he was shook.

"Listen, Wylie," Earl he choked, "I believe you, so let's get outta here."

"Skeered, boys," the Arkie said and it wasn't no question.

"Like hell," said Big Duncan that won't admit he's a-scared of nothin', 'specially stuff that has him flat terrified.

7

"Looks like to me you boys're fixin' to crawfish, see," challenged Wylie.

Now I know Dunc don't have a hair on his ass, he just talks big. But, as a matter a fact, I was ready to crawfish, so I cinched up my butt, and I fired back at him real indignant: "Hell no, you big turkey! You're a-fuckin' with your pulse when you call me chickenshit!" I couldn't let no sumbitch think I was scared, 'specially since I was.

That's what took us another fifty yards farther into dark trees with what looked like hangin' vines and fallen limbs and water slidin' by, darker all the time, nobody talkin' or hardly breathin'. Then Bob Don Bundy he let out a war-whoop: "Snaaaaaake!" He danced some steps ol' Fred Astaire never mastered.

The Arkie, he flashed his light and I spit at Bob Don — my own heart was poundin' like a damn congo drum — "That ain't nothin' but a damn piece a rope!" But it was all coiled up like a snake, and right next to the trail too; it did look like a snake. Folks don't hardly ever leave coils a rope out in the middle of nowheres. That vexed me some.

Wasn't but thirty or forty yards farther and Earl howled, "It's got me! Oh Lord, it's got me!" His voice it had turned soprano and he was jerkin' and jumpin'. Whenever we got a-holt to him, he was whiter'n a accountant's legs. We calmed him down some — all of us breathin' purty heavy too — and we untangled his trousers from the bob-wire some fool had went and strung across the trail. Earl he was shakin' like a virgin at the drive-in movie.

"Skeered, girls?" challenged Dunc.

"Hose you, Duncan!" snapped Earl. "Let's get outta here."

"Somebody's gonna knock a lung outta you, Duncan," I warned.

Big Dunc just give me this tight grin.

8

Me, I was fixin' to agree with Earl, then ol' Wylie he tossed his two bits' worth in: "Fixin' to twist off, boys?" That done 'er! "Hell no! You and yer boy Duncan 're about to get turned ever' which way but loose, though! Now let's go find that big bad gator!" No way I was a-gonna let them two peckerheads know I was suckin' wind with my ass.

Not ten strides up the trail, Big Dunc the buttless wonder he fell in that hole. He never give a pip, but he must of left his courage in there whenever he climbed out, because if he'd of had any ass he'd a been a-haulin' it back to Oildale. The big guy was movin'. We never seen no more a him that night. "There goes the bravest man in Kern County," I said, "worthless as a piss sandwich."

Earl he never paid me no mind. "Lord," he gasped, "that's a gator hole sure as anything."

"*A gator hole?*" whined Bob Don. If his voice got any higher only a dog could a-heard him.

To me it just looked like somebody'd went and dug a pit, so I snorted, "Come on!"

We crept a bit farther till we come to a spot where the river widened and flattened so it looked almost like a bayou.

"This here's the very place I seen that gator, boys," Wylie he announced.

"Where's it at?" I demanded.

"Well, I don't know rightly," the ol' Arkie he admitted, rubbin' his chin that always had spots a whiskers bristlin' from it like bunchgrass on account of him never shavin' too precise. "Around here somewheres I reckon."

"You mean you brought us clean out here and you don't even know where that gator is? Just what I figured, a damn lie." What with bein' so tense, I got right away mad. "You're apt a get a dent knocked in your dick pullin' this little stunt!"

"Here," Wylie said, handin' me his flashlight. "You find it. They do move around. They got legs, and they swim, too, ya know."

9

That remark liked to cost Wylie what was left of his teeth, but instead I just jerked it out of his hand and moved the beam around the water. Nothin'. Just when I was fixin' to crown Wylie with his light, somethin' *did* glint close to shore, so I flashed the beam toward it and — Lord have mercy! — two big red eyes they shone back at me.

I knocked Bob Don ass over teakettle when I spun around and exploded up the trail. Wasn't nothin' short of a- runnin' right into a giant redwood could of slowed me down, 'cause I was pickin' 'em up and layin' 'em down, boys. Then damned if Earl he didn't pass me. But not for long. I cut in the afterburner and flew right by him. Bob Don he was behind us, and I heard him screechin', "What *is* it? What *is* it?"

I run so fast that I passed Wylie's broke down ol' pickup too. I wasn't waitin' for that ol' boy. I wasn't waitin' for nobody. I was headed O-U-T out! And fast.

Me and Earl we was on our second beers, inhalin' them devils, whenever ol' Wylie's truck it pulled up to the Tejon Club. He dumped Bob Don off — the college graduate lookin' flat sick, eyes like broke eggs — then waved and pulled away. I never waved back because it looked like to me he was laughin' at us. I finished my beer and asked ol' Larry for another'n.

Next day after work while it was still light me and Earl we took our shotguns out there to hunt that gator, but we never seen it. "Prob'ly swum off lookin' for warmer water," Earl suggested.

I only nodded, 'cause I'd saw a couple a bicycle reflectors tacked on a log there in the bushes, and marks where it'd been dragged out of the water and hid by somebody. I'd saw and thought about it too. Thought hard.

"Okay, Wylie," I said to myself, already schemin' my revenge, "that's how we're a-playin' her, eh? Oky-doky, Wylie. Oky-doky. You're in a world of trouble now!" ▮

The Call of the
Great Frog King

He's a smart sucker, Bob Don Bundy. Hell, he even wears a necktie to work, that's how come us boys we took him serious whenever he told us his plan. See, it wasn't but a couple weeks since that lame-brained Wylie Hillis had went and tricked us with a fake alligator in the Kern River. Well, ol' Wylie he never knew the kinda guys he was a-messin' with, I'll tell you that much. He was a-playin' in the big leagues whenever he played with us, by damn.

Us boys we was settin' around the Tejon Club havin' this deep discussion about monster truck rallies that afternoon whenever it dawned on me that Big Dunc and Earl that run the joint, they still hadn't figgered out the trick. Me, I'd seen them bike reflectors tacked on a log and I'd told Bob Don about 'em. Course, you can't expect Duncan and Earl to figger things out as good as Bob Don. They never graduated Bakersfield Junior College like him.

Anyways, after we'd switched to wrestlin' on TV, we took to discussin' who was the dirtiest villain we ever seen — "That Mr. Moto, he used to *kill* guys with his Japan sleep hold," Earl argued. Then ol' Duncan he ups and says real thoughtful, "Why do you suppose there aren't *more* gators in the river? I mean, if there's one, there might could be a whole *mess* of 'em, see."

"Well," answered Bob Don Bundy, the junior-college graduate, winkin' at me, "that cold water froze their nuts off so they couldn't breed."

Dunc's eyes narrowed. "Is that right?" he said.

"Yeah," Bob Don went on, soundin' mighty solemn, like maybe he's a personal friend of the nutless gator, "it's kind of like nature's birth control, otherwise there'd be gators all over the river just snapping up all the drunks from L.A. floating downstream on inner tubes."

The big guy he seemed fascinated by all this nature stuff. "Is that a fact?" he repeated.

I couldn't help but laugh, 'specially when Earl he rolled that soggy toothpick around his mouth and said, "Hell, if they'll eat them L.A.-types, I might buy 'em all nut-warmers so they *can* breed."

The rest of us, we was laughin' to beat hell, specially since Earl'd went and suggested he might *buy* anything. He's still chokin' ol' George Washington on the first buck he ever earned.

"A couple a you peckerheads're fixin' to get your asses kicked, see," growled the big man. Dunc's little eyes blinked, and he finally seemed to catch on that we was raggin' him. "Get one a them ball-warmer deals for yerself, Bundy," he added, "a real littleun, see."

"Duncan," I finally said, "you got the easiest cage to rattle in the Kern County." I explained to him and Earl how Wylie'd went and fooled us. At first they never believed me, but purty soon Big Dunc he said, "Why that ol' farmer! How's come him to pull that crap? Somebody might just have to kick his ass, see."

12

"I b'lieve he resented the time he brung the missus in here, Dunc, and you commenced that virtuoso fartin' exhibition," I suggested.

Earl nodded and fluttered his ever-present toothpick. "He did look a tad pissed that time, didn't he?"

"Thin-skinned sumbitch, ain't he. Why them A-rabs, they think a fart's right neighborly, see," added Duncan.

"Wylie isn't an Arab," Bob Don pointed out.

"His missus, she looked flat embarrassed," I said.

Dunc grinned real evil. "She looked just plain flat to me, see."

"A lotta difference that'd make to Wylie," said Earl. "Hell, his horse's been dead so long he doesn't even have to lock the barn anymore." His toothpick danced whenever he laughed.

That give us a kick, and Bob Don he added, "What can't get up can't get out."

But Dunc, as per usual, he set there a minute grindin' at bein' tricked, then got hisself pissed. "You wait'll that ol' Arkie comes in here, see, I'll kick his ass so hard he'll have to take his hat off to shit."

"Cool off, Duncan," urged Bob Don. "Cool off. I've got a better idea. Why don't we give Mr. Hillis a taste of his own medicine? Why don't we just trick Mr. Tricky."

Me and Earl right away agreed. Hell, it sounded like fun to me. But Big Dunc he never looked too sure until Bob Don pulled this newspaper clippin' from his pocket and said, "Listen to this: 'Officials of the Department of Fish and Game are seeking means to combat the spread of the African Swamp Frog. This large, aggressive exotic is spreading into California from Mexico. It devours native bullfrogs and displaces them in the ecosystem. A full-sized adult male may be three times the size of the largest bullfrog.'"

There's more," said Bob Don, but that's the important part."

13

"So what?" asked Dunc that wasn't the brightest bastard to come down the pike.

Bob Don looked at me and Earl. "You guys get it, don't you?"

We never.

Bundy he made this clickin' sound with his mouth, then asked real slow, "Who likes to gig frogs more than anyone in Kern County?"

"Why, Wylie Hillis," I replied, still not gettin' it.

"That's right," smiled Bob Don, "Wylie Hillis. And who can we trick out into the swamp and scare the crap out of if we tell him there're giant frogs out there?"

"Wylie Hillis!" I snapped, finally catchin' on, "And I already got me an idea how." I may not've graduated Bakersfield Junior College like Bob Don done, but I'm half-smart myownself. That's why I recollected this guy I'd knew in high school. His real name was Albert, but none of us called him that. Nope, we called him the Great Frog King.

He could make the best fart sounds in Oildale — with his armpit, I mean. He wasn't firin' the real McCoy the way Duncan always did. Yessir, the King he could croak them devils out like frogs in the rain: He'd stick his left hand under his shirt and cup it in his right pit, crook his right arm, then pump that sucker like a one-winged goose tryin' to take off. And lord the sounds he could make!

I'll tell you somethin' else: The Great Frog King he wasn't just talented, he's a smart sucker hisownself. He won the damn spellin' bee at the high school and he liked to've made the honor roll to boot. And he was a athlete too: He could shoot pool as good as anybody in our class. But even in the pool hall it's them sounds made him famous. I recollect how he played "Peg O' My Heart" with his armpit that time in study hall. He even tried to enter the high school talent contest but this mean teacher she wouldn't let him.

14

Naturally, I thought of the King whenever Bob Don he mentioned them frogs. And Bob Don he was real impressed with my idea: "He sounds perfect. Maybe we can get him to lure Wylie out into the boonies, then we can dump him. That'll teach him."

"I'd rather stomp him, see," said Duncan.

"No, Dunc," said Bob Don real persuasive, "we're all agreed that we'll trick him back. There'll be no *need* to work him over when we're done with him. Now here's what we can do..."

Every time ol' Wylie he come in the Tejon Club for a beer after that, us boys we commenced talkin' about these great big huge frogs we been seein' in the Kern River. We never talked d'rectly *to* him, of course, we just gabbed real loud to each other, and we could see his big leathery ol' ears kinda flap in our direction, him a-takin' the bait slow but sure just like Bob Don predicted.

"Yessir," I announced to Big Dunc, "the size of a badger it was. If a guy could gig one a them suckers, he'd have frog legs enough for Thanksgivin' dinner."

"No shit," said Dunc real thoughtful.

"Is that right?" Earl piped in.

Bob Don had went and posted that there frog article he'd read us on the bulletin board near the door. I seen ol' Wylie look it over real close. Then Bob Don, clever like always, he printed up this official-lookin' announcement in the office where he worked, and he posted it there on the board too. Ol' Wylie he give thatun a real good look-see too.

Meanwhile, I'd got in touch with my ol' buddy, the Great Frog King, and he was hot to go along with the joke. In fact, what he done was stick his hand into his armpit and pump out a couple a sea-lion barks. "How're those for African frogs?" he asked with a big grin.

"Perfect." I said. "Just perfect." I was a-rubbin' my hands at the thought of ol' Wylie Hillis gettin' his comeuppance. Boy, ol' Albert the King sure hadn't lost none of his talent, even if he was a bookkeeper now.

When everything was set, we sprung the trap on that ol'Arkie. Wylie, he come slouchin' into the Tejon Club that afternoon and ordered him a beer. We'd all showed up early that day and poured even more beer down our throats than usual waitin' for the chump to show up, so I can tell you we was real loose by the time he did.

Once ol' Hillis'd set a spell, Bob Don announced just loud enough, "Well, boys, it looks like a perfect night for frogging."

"Yeah," I answered just like we'd planned, "but we better bring heavy-duty equipment if we're goin' after them big suckers."

"That's for sure," added Earl.

Wylie, he eyed Dunc that hadn't said nothin', then asked real casual, "Goin' froggin', boys?"

"Yeah, we thought we just might kill the night that way," replied Bob Don Bundy, slick as snot.

Easy does it, I was thinkin'. Since we'd already drove ol' Albert out to the ambush spot and fortified him with a pint of Four Roses whiskey to fight the chill, I didn't want to warn Wylie Hillis off. "We ain't had no frog legs to eat for awhile," I added, "and a few a them devils'd sure taste semi-good."

"That's for sure," agreed Earl. He sounded like a bad actor readin' lines, so I give him the evil eye.

Wylie he looked at his beer and said, "I hope you boys ain't still sore over that little alligator deal I pulled on ya."

I was thinkin' *you'll find out how sore I am, you ol' fartknocker*, but I just smiled and said, "Us? Sore? Heck a mile, Wylie, fun's fun."

Bob Don was grinnin'. "Hey, we appreciate a joke as much as the next person does. Don't we Dunc?"

The big guy was hunched over his beer there at the bar, his ass crack exposed to wind and rain. He stared straight ahead at the big jar of pickled pigs' feet on the counter, his eyes lookin' like a taxidermist just inserted 'em.

"*Right, Dunc!*" insisted Bob Don.

"Yeah," the big guy finally grunted, the veins on his forearms knottin' underneath them fadin' tattoos. He wasn't too good a actor either.

"Well, I'm surely happy to hear it," smiled Wylie real friendly. "I'd sure like to join y'all for a little froggin', specially since you're a-goin' after them big Afercan bastards."

"You sure can," Earl sang out right away, and I give him the high sign; hell, he's gonna give the whole thing away bein' so obvious.

But Wylie never caught on, the simple bastard, and before long us boys was out on the sidewalk talkin' frogs. He was stubborn, though, insistin' on takin' his own pickup, sayin' he had to go home and fetch his waders and gig. It didn't matter. We took a bag a beer with us, killin' a few more a them bad boys on our way to the Kern River. We had the ol' boy right where we wanted him.

It had went and turned dark by the time we got out there, us parkin' in almost exactly the same place as whenever ol' Wylie'd made trouble for hisself by trickin' us. Well, by damn, the worm was fixin' to turn, so us boys had us a good laugh, discussin' our plan and tossin' the empties into the bushes soon as we drained 'em waitin' on the guest of honor.

Once he arrived, we all trooped through them trees and vines for a damn mile, carryin' our sack and gigs and lights and waders, and totin' a pretty good beer supply in us, so we had to stop and water the trees pretty regular. Finally, we reached that little swampy pond that was part of the river's overflow.

"Where them gi'nt frogs at, *Perfesssor?*" asked Wylie.

"Oh, they're off in the danged bog," explained Bob Don. "We're going to have to wade a little."

17

"Good enough," replied the ol' fart.

Bob Don he whispered to me, "Where's your pal the Frog King? I thought he was supposed to give us a concert."

A little stung, I insisted, "He *will*." But I was wonderin' myownself.

Ol' Earl, that subtle bastard, he damn near hollered, "I sure hope we *hear* some frogs d'rectly," tryin' to wake ol' Albert up I guess.

In fact, we was hearin' nothin' *but* frogs, but only the usual Kern River kind.

Big Dunc that hadn't been sayin' nothin' he finally chimed in: "Anybody bring some beer? I'm gettin' thirsty, see." I think he was also gettin' scared. He's a big chickenshit.

"Now don't use your flashlight, boys, until we're right next to those giant African frogs," advised Bob Don. "We don't want to scare them."

"Gi'nt Afercan?" gasped Dunc like he just realized what we was up to. He was a damn caution, that guy.

Still there wasn't no sound from the Great Frog King, that peckerhead.

Well, we sloshed through them creepy reeds and weeds, up to our ankles in water, up to our asses in beer, everythin' gettin' darker 'n' darker. Us boys, we acted like we was ready to gig some big giant African frogs, but we was really more interested in giggin' Wylie Hillis...and the damn Frog King if he didn't get started. Me, I was beginnin' to wonder if givin' him that bottle of Four Roses was such a good plan. "Maybe a pint was too much for ol' Albert," I whispered to Bob Don, but he only shushed me.

"I surely don't see no big frogs," pronounced Wylie, beginnin' to sound dubious.

Me, I was beginnin' to wear out on the deal myself; that beer it was sloshin' around in me and the good time had lost its edge.

"They're just up ahead," said Bob Don, not soundin' too convincin' even to me. That damned Albert had went and wrecked our plan.

Just then Wylie he kinda veered off to the left and, in that dark, I couldn't see him a-tall. "Hey!" I called, but he never answered. That tore things! There we was out in the damn boonies, wet, beer turnin' sour, and our plan about shot. Now the victim had took off. I stopped, but Bob Don hissed, "Keep going, J.B. Maybe we can at least strand the old bird out here."

At last, Albert he finally come through. From off in the distance, we heard this kinda metallic "Ou-gah! Ou-gah!" — the call of the Great Frog King! I knew we was finally in business.

Duncan he tilted his head like a dog hearin' a siren, and said, "What the hell?" his voice quiverin'.

"Ou-gah! Ou-gah!" come that call again. It wasn't like any frog I'd ever heard. Leave it to ol' Albert to come up with a new one. Me and Bob Don we grinned at each other in the dark.

There wasn't no way Wylie could miss that there sound, or resist it either. No way. We had him now. We was in muck halfway up to our knees by then, almost to a little rise or island surrounded by cattails, a place we'd went froggin' before. There was this low, smoky mist comin' up from the wet around it. That was exactly where we'd left the Frog King with the Four Roses, but it sounded like he'd moved to a better spot. Like I told you, he damn near made the honor roll back in high school so he was smart. "Ou-gah! Ou-gah!"

"That *is* Albert, right?" whispered Earl.

"Hush," I warned, "or you'll give the trick away." Wylie wasn't nowhere to be seen, but he could be right next to us for all I knew.

We hoofed through reeds and rushes onto the high ground and it come clear that the Frog King'd moved into a swampy area right in front of us. I figured him to be hidin' in the reeds there. I never seen him, but I surely heard that "Ou-gah! Ou-gah!" I was lookin' all around for Wylie Hillis because I knew he had to be closin' in too, but I couldn't see him. We still hadn't flipped on our flashlights since you can see better without 'em after you get used to the dark.

But Dunc and Earl both looked ready to switch theirs on anyways, holdin' 'em like rifles. I started to tell 'em to keep their fingers off them switches whenever I stumbled. "Key-rist!" I spit.

"What's wrong?" asked Bob Don real concerned.

"I tripped over this damned log..." I started to tell 'em, then it moaned. I looked close and it wasn't no log. It was the Great Frog King all curled around that empty bottle of Four Roses. While me and the other boys was lookin' down at him, we heard, "Ou-gah! Ou-gah!" comin' from right ahead of us.

"What the heck?" wondered Bob Don.

"Then who's...?" asked Earl.

"Oh shit!," groaned Big Dunc, and four flashlight beams popped on at once.

I swung mine toward where I thought I'd heard that sound comin' from, and I noticed somethin' pushin' toward us through the cattails, a kinda big blunt deal movin' real slow like a gopher snake after a mouse. Even with my light on, I couldn't make it out real good, but it damn sure got my attention.

"What's that?" asked Bob Don, his voice a octave higher.

"Ohhh shit," said Dunc and he turned around and commenced hoofin' away. But I grabbed his arm. "Hold on," I said.

"Ou-gah!" come that roar d'rectly from that blunt deal that was a-pushin' through them reeds toward us, and I jumped pretty good. Bob Don and Earl was quiverin' but they held their ground.

I squinted real hard tryin' to recognize what the hell that deal was. Then I seen them eyes, huge white ones a-gapin' at us through that low fog and tules.

Eyes! That big blunt deal had eyes!

Dunc seen 'em too. He was turnin' whenever he said, "It's the Gi'nt Afercan Frog, see!" He was in full stride by the time the last words was finished — "Plop! Plop! Plop!" his waders almost explodin' as he run — and let me tell ya, that big booger was *movin'*.

Me, I was right on his heels. I never knew for sure what that blunt deal was, but I wasn't gonna stick around to find out either. Just my luck, I stumbled over that damn Albert sprawled on the ground, and I was right there next to him with that blunt deal movin' toward us.

Big Dunc, though, he was just gettin' unlimbered. He bowled over Bob Don that'd took off first without me noticin', and they both sailed about twenty foot before they landed. Earl he took to spinnin' his wheels, spirit willin' but waders not cooperatin'. His eyes looked about like them frog's. Meanwhile Bob Don he took to howlin' that the frog had bit his tail and he's damn near climbin' Dunc tryin' to get to goin' again.

I was back on my feet by then, but I wasn't waitin' for nobody, 'specially not no Giant African Frog. I whizzed by Dunc and Bob Don, them lookin' like mud wrestlers, and seen that the latter had gigged his own ass in the spill so he had a pole hangin' from him like a tadpole's tail. Ol' Earl he finally got goin' about then, and he give me a good race back to the truck, but he never beat me.

Me and him we was puffin' there leanin' on the truck — our flashlights and gigs lost back in the bog — me holdin' a tire iron I'd took from the tool box just in case that blunt deal'd followed us. Then we heard what sounded like a damn elephant stampede — "Plop! Plop! Plop!" — so we ducked down and I raised that iron, but it was only Bob Don and Dunc, all brown with mud so they looked like they was in one of them damn menstrual shows, a-sprintin' in. Bundy he'd somehow lost his waders.

"What *was* that thing?" asked Bob Don.

"It'uz a damn gi'nt Afercan deal, see," puffed Duncan. "I seen it with my own eyes."

Safe back at the pickup, my breath startin' to come regular, I had me the same question. "Well," I said, "if that really *is* a Giant African Frog, the King's been et by now and good riddance."

"Let's get outta here and talk about it at the club," suggested Earl that had his eyes scannin' down the trail we'd run.

Bob Don he was rubbin' his ass where he'd gigged hisself, and moanin' while he looked back at them dark woods.

"Well, what's the plan *now?*," I asked him real sarcastic.

"Somethin's comin'!" said Earl real tense. "Listen!"

"What? Where?" asked Dunc, then he took off for Oildale — "Plop! Plop! Plop!" — movin' as fast as his waders'd take him. Earl he stood there turnin' his head like he was watchin' a tennis game, not sure whether to join Duncan or stay with us. Brave Bob Don started to climb into the truck's cab, but he dropped his keys and commenced scramblin' around the ground there in the dark tryin' real desperate to find 'em. Me, I squatted down behind the cab again and raised that tire iron; I was fixin' to put a dent in that sucker if it come for me.

Then we heard that voice: "Git any frogs, boys?" It was that ol' Arkie Wylie Hillis.

He never waited for no answer. "I got me a mess a big bullfrogs but I never seen no Gi'nt Afercans." He held up his gunny sack and I seen a big lump in its bottom. "What happened to you, *Perfesssor?*" he asked Bob Don.

The college graduate looked up from the ground, halfway under his truck, "Nothing!" he spit. "Let's go." He wasn't in no mood to talk to Wylie Hillis.

"You sound a tad touchy, there, *Perfesssor*. Wasn't it you that said fun's fun? Well, I just had me a good time a-giggin' these frogs."

"What about Albert?" asked Earl that'd calmed down a tad.

"To heck with him!" Bundy snapped. He'd found his keys and he was ready to haul ass. He climbed up into the cab and sit down as gentle as he could.

"Albert?" asked the ol' Arkie.

While they talked, I wandered toward Wylie's pickup to look at the frogs in the sack he'd threw into the bed, and I noticed this big box. Wrote on it was "United States Government Surplus Inflatable Two-Man Raft, One Each." I lifted this tarp next to it and I seen a couple of small cans of paint and some brushes.

Well, I never told the other boys what I seen, but I sure as hell thought about it. On the way back to the Tejon Club, I figgered out what had to've happened and I said to myself, "Okay, Wylie," already layin' a scheme for revenge. "Oky-doky!"

That ol' Arkie he was in the *world* of trouble now, by damn! ▤

The Great Oildale Bee-In

See Big Dunc settin' over there a-grinnin' like a dead possum and with all them folks around him buyin' him beers? Naw, he ain't serious hurt. All them bandages show is there ain't no damn justice. Hell, I'm a-itchin' hornet bites all over me and I ain't wearin' no damn bandages. Fact is, if it wasn't for Dunc that caused the fracas in the first place, wouldn't none of us be itchin' these damn bites, but *that* fartknocker's collectin' the free beers. The whole thing started, as per usual, with him runnin' his mouth.

"It's the damn commonists, is who," he announced, tryin' to change the topic from that sorry excuse for a mustache he'd took to sportin'.

"Wash your lip, Duncan," said Bob Don.

"Eat shit. They brung in them damn killer bees and put 'em right here in Kern County on account of we're all patriots hereabouts, not damn liberals. It's like them damn no-smokin' laws. Gimme a refill, Earl."

The proprietor, he narrowed his eyes at Dunc and his toothpick pointed at him. Earl he'd quit smokin' a couple years before, and he'd told everyone no more smokin' in his joint because he didn't wanta be around it. Well, Duncan he'd pissed and moaned, but not to Earl, and except for a few newcomers, nobody'd smoked in the club since then that I know of — the only cigarette-free poolhall in the world, I bet. "If you wanta go drink somewheres else, Duncan..." Earl suggested.

"Damn, but you're gettin' touchy," grunted Dunc. "How 'bout that beer?"

Earl drew another draft for Dunc, commentin', "Besides, that thing looks like a caterpillar died on your lip."

Dunc the patriot ignored him; he wasn't finished with his lecture: "And that ain't all," he went on, "you know them killer watermelons that they come from right here in Kern County, your commonists done that too, see."

"Is that a fact?" observed Wylie Hillis.

"You damn rights."

"You mean the ones that farmers contaminated with pesticide?" asked Bob Don.

"They never. It was them commonists, see."

"It looks like some damn *public* hair growin' over your mouth," I told him. Dunc's one a them great big guys that don't have much whiskers, so his sorry excuse for a mustache really was a sight.

"Eat shit," he snorted at me. "And that damn killer water in the wells that it's supposed to be the farmers' fault; well, the commonists done that to scare us workin' guys, see. It's your liberal medias that spread them lies," Duncan announced. "Them and that damn Sahara Club."

Bob Don Bundy, who's a smart sucker because he graduated Bakersfield Junior College, he spoke up: "*Sierra* Club, Dunc, and it seems to me I read that those bees came up from South America on some oilfield equipment."

"*Read!*" spat Dunc that rarely looked at more than tit magazines. "Hell, your commies they control your liberal medias, see."

"That's a true fact!" agreed Wylie Hillis that usually never got along too good with Dunc. He had his corncob pipe — unlit, of course, clamped in his teeth. "I read it in this deal that Olive she brung home from church that it tells the true facts."

"I thought you just read them *style* magazines, Wylie," I couldn't help sayin'. He had on his usual pair of old, zip-up coveralls, a crumpled red ballcap that said "Copenhagen" on it, and scuffed up cowboy boots. I figured he was just waitin' on some guy from *Gentlemen's Quarterly* to rush over and take his picture.

"How do you know a communist didn't write *that* tract, Wylie, just to trick you?" asked Bob Don.

There was dead silence in the Tejon Club as the ol' Arkie blinked at Dunc, and Dunc blinked back at him. Finally, the big guy came up with a snappy reply, "Eat shit, Bob Don."

Bundy he grinned and winked at me and Earl.

"Well la-tee-da Mr. Big Britches!" Wylie added, his wrinkled old face screwed up till it looked about like a road apple. "Olive she taken it from the table right in the Assembly of God and ain't no red commonist a-goin' in there without lightnin' blowin' their balls off."

"Damn rights," said Duncan.

"Well," I said, "whoever put them bees here, we better watch ourselves because lookee here." I snapped open the *Bakersfield Californian* and showed the boys that headline: "Killer Bees Found in Oildale."

"No shit?" said Earl.

"Where'bouts?" asked Dunc, real tense.

"It says they found a hive of 'em in a pipe out in the old Kern River oilfield," I explained. "It says they could be anywheres."

"Anywheres?" said Wylie Hillis, his eyes buggin' out. He looked around the club real careful. "What's that thang?" he demanded, pointing at something buzzin' around the front window.

"I believe that's a killer fly," Earl said, and me and Bob Don laughed.

Dunc never. He had this real serious look on his face. "I might just have to go out to take care a them killer bees myself. I'm a veteran, ya know."

"I recollect when you fought the war in a supply room at Fort Ord, Dunc," I pointed out, "so don't give me that veteran shit like you'uz in Ko-rea or Viet-nam. You never even got a Good Conduct Medal."

"Well, if I hadn't socked that damn sergeant, I'd'a got me one. Anyways, I'm a damn trained killer, see."

"Yeah, Dunc," I said, a-winkin' at Bob Don. "I noticed the commies never took over California while you'uz at Fort Ord issuin' drawers to new recruits."

"Damn rights," burped Dunc, then he slurped up some more brew. "It'uz a rough deal, see," he conceded.

"Well," Bob Don finally said, his tone a little deeper, "first of all, those aren't `killer bees,' they're really just an Africanized strain that's a bit more aggressive..."

"*Afercan*," Wylie Hillis snorted. "You could figger *coloreds* to be in on it!"

"Speakin' a that," said Earl, "young Jeffrey's comin' in to help me clean up today and I don't want nobody sayin' `colored' in front of him."

Me and Heddy, my wife that teaches at Beardsley School, we'd heard that this little colored kid and his momma was livin' in that project over by Beardsley, and that they was havin' a tough time makin' ends meet on account of the momma she was sick. So I'd proposed to

Earl that we invent a after-school job for the kid. Well, that ol' tightwad he'd hemmed and hawed, chewin' on that toothpick — "How much you figure somethin' like that might run me?" — and I said me and Heddy'd pay for it, so he said okay. But Earl that ain't got no boys of his own, he took to Jeffrey right away, and now he's chippin' in and so are all the other regulars — all but cept Wylie, anyways — to pay the kid for cleanin' up around the place.

Just to be a smart-ass, Dunc asked, "What if somebody was to say `colored' but they never meant it, see?" He was grinnin' real evil.

Earl he took that sawed-off pool cue from underneath the bar and patted one open hand with it. "What if I was to tap somebody with this attitude adjuster, lower their hairline a foot or two...but I never meant it?" he asked.

Dunc he just kept grinnin'.

Bob Don ignored us and just kept on talkin' like we'd never even interrupted him: "Anyway, they're Africanized but since there're so many more domestic bees around here, it won't take long for the gene pool to absorb their aggressive tendencies and calm them down."

Well, that made good sense to me. I mean, we got thousands of commercial beehives here in Kern County on account of because the farmers they use them to pollinate their crops. "Yeah," I agreed.

"Gene pool? What the hell's that?" demanded Dunc.

"It's something you swim in the shallow end of," Bob Don whispered out of the corner of his mouth.

"Anyways, that's just the kinda deal them commie medias want ya to think, see," Big Dunc asserted.

"How do you know so much about the medias?" asked Earl that knew Dunc never read nothin' voluntarily, cept maybe *Boobs International* and *Bottoms Up*.

"It just happens that the War Department"—that's how he called his wife Dee Dee—"she brung home a deal from church too that tells the true facts, that's how!" the big guy snorted. "And them damn commies they made a mistake whenever they brung them bees down thisaway. I got a way of dealin' with 'em that works, by damn, and" — he turned to face me — "it'll just interest you, Mr. Jerry Bill never-even-been-in-the-army, to know that I *learned* it in the army, see. I made me a damn flame thrower."

Me and Bob Don looked at each other and grinned. Earl laughed out loud. "You made *what?*" he said.

"A damn flame-thrower deal is what."

"That oughta get 'em," ol' Wylie he piped up.

"It sounds like your basic overkill to me," observed Bob Don.

I seen Dunc and Wylie blink at each other again, then Wylie he said, "Well, that's a good deal. The missus one time she got stung by a damn bee and swole all up, had to go to the damn doctor is where! Them're danger's critters, bees."

"Hell, ol' Dunc oughta let one sting him. He'd like to swell up for a change. And his ol' lady'd *really* like him to."

"Eat shit," said Dunc that's got a golden tongue when it comes to slick answers.

"What would we do with *your* clothes when we finished?" asked Bob Don.

Silence again. Finally Dunc narrowed them BBs he uses for eyes. "Meanin' what, see?" he hissed.

Bob Don smiled. "Nothing."

"You better hope one of them bees doesn't crawl in your coveralls with you, Wylie," I couldn't resist addin'. "He might like it in there real cozy, but I bet you wouldn't."

Wylie right away pulled his zipper up even higher and eyed that killer fly on the window.

"Well, I gotta take off," Big Dunc said. "If you boys see any a them killer bees, just give me a call, see. Me and my flame-thrower deal'll take good care of 'em."

"It's good to have a veteran around," said Bob Don with a wink.

"Damn rights," Dunc grunted, not smilin'.

"Well, if I see any," winked Earl, "I'll damn sure let you know. It'll be like callin' in the damn *calvary!*" He grinned.

"You'll think calvary whenever I get done with 'em, see..." challenged the big guy.

"I'd surely be proud to see that there flame-thrower deal a yours," said Wylie, Dunc's new buddy.

The big guy he perked right up. "Why hell yeah. Come on by the place and I'll show it to ya, see."

"Sure thang."

Well, them two they took off, goin' to search for some "communist bees" or "killer medias," I reckoned. I suggested that to Earl and Bob Don, and they liked to fell on the floor laughin'. Then Bob Don he got this big huge grin on his face, and he said, "What do you say we just see that they find some?"

I looked at Earl and he looked at me, and we both grinned ourownselves. "Damn rights," I said.

Dunc come in that next afternoon and ordered him a brew. From the way he was a-settin', all hunched over, I think he was ready for us to start in on his lip hair, but instead I said, "Did you hear that program on the radio about killer bees?"

"What's that?" he asked.

"Well, it said they make a nest by pluggin' up one end of a pipe with mud, and you can tell if it's them by all these little holes stuck in the mud — that's how they go in and out."

"Oh yeah," said Earl that he was in on the scheme, "I heard that too. It said the best time to get 'em is early in the mornin' before they take to flyin'."

Bob Don chimed in then. "Yeah, and they're really silent; you can't even hear them buzzing in the pipe, but they're there. And it said no other animal makes a nest like that one. The announcer said they're easy to identify, and that people in Oildale have to be especially careful. You just look for a pipe blocked with mud that's got a bunch of little holes about like a pencil'd been stuck in it."

"What is?" It was Wylie Hillis that'd just walked in while we was talkin'. We repeated the story and I seen his old eyes bulge. He looked real concerned, just like we'd hoped.

"Well, after I fry them bastards with my flamethrower deal," our hero announced, "they won't bother nobody, see."

"That's a fact!" Wylie he chimed in. "Ol' Dunc here he showed me and he's damn sure made him one."

While we was talkin' that afternoon, my boy Craig and his pal Junior and little Jeffrey that they'd kind of adopted, they was doin' this little task I'd set 'em to. See, ol' Wylie's a packrat, never throws nothin' away, so his yard's full of junk: a couple old cars, used lumber, some rusted oil drums, and of course a mess of pipes. Them two boys, they plugged up three of them pipes with mud and poked lotsa holes in the plugs with pencils, then skedaddled before Miz Hillis could get home from the Assembly of God, where she hung out most afternoons, and catch 'em.

It never took long. That night I got a call from Earl. "They took the bait. Ol' Wylie's scared shitless, so Big Dunc the war hero's gonna bring his flame thrower first thing in the mornin'. I already called Bob Don. We're gonna meet for coffee at Lorene's Cafe at five, then go over to Wylie's."

"Hey, I'll be there."

We beat Dunc to Hillis's place — me, Earl, and Bob Don. Wylie he come out from the house and joined us then, directly; the war hero hisself wheeled his pickup into the driveway and climbed out. He was wearin' these real tight army fatigues — his old ones, I'd guess, since the sleeves never had nothin' on 'em, but you could see where

31

one chevron had been sewed on and tore off. His belly it was peekin' between buttons and makin' a real good attempt at buryin' his belt. He looked flat silly to me.

He was all business, though. He turned and grabbed this fancy rig from the truck's bed. It was a butane tank with a long hose attached and a metal rod on the end. There was shoulder straps on the tank, and a valve on top.

Bob Don poked me. "Leave it to Dunc. No way he can turn that thing on when he's wearing it."

He was right. Dunc climbed into his gear, then said to Wylie, "Okay, you walk behind me, see, so's you can turn 'er on whenever I say to."

"*Me?*" Wylie's voice it went real high and us guys couldn't hardly keep from laughin' out loud. His pipe was lit and it began smokin' like a steam engine.

"Aren't you gonna wear glasses or somethin' to protect your face, Duncan," asked Earl that'd did lots of work with fire in the oilfields before he bought the Tejon Club.

Big Dunc he couldn't hide his scorn. "I ain't chickenshit, like some, see," he spit. "I'm a damn veteran."

"Yeah, well all those professional firemen'll be glad to hear they don't need the masks they've been wearin'," Earl spit out in a tone that said *stupid bastard* better'n the words could.

Dunc never wanted to tangle with Earl that run the club so he shut up and edged up toward one of the pipes the boys had plugged, the snout of his flame thrower extended out in front toward that nest. Wylie he was laggin' along way behind him, and the big guy hissed, "Keep up, see!"

Wylie looked back at us, and his face looked about like he was bein' drug to the damn electrical chair. While Dunc waited, the ol' boy caught up real reluctant. Then them two crept closer, closer, closer. Finally, the war hero he stopped and stuck that flame thrower's snout as far in front of him as it'd go, almost up to the killer nest. "Turn it on, see," he ordered Wylie, who reached up, opened the valve of the tank on Dunc's back and scuttled back toward us as fast as he could.

After a second, Dunc flipped a switch and "WHOMP!" come a giant blue flash like somebody's lit one massive fart, then the flame thrower it petered out.

All of us guys we was knocked back a step, and Duncan was flattened like ol' Cassius Clay had went and socked him. We was all laughin' to beat hell, all but cept Wylie that is. Me, I was still gigglin' whenever I felt a hot sting on my wrist, another on my neck, then another'n on my cheek.

About then, I heard Wylie let out a war-whoop: "KILLER BEES! IT'S KILLER BEES!" And he took off. Lemme tell ya, that ol' boy could motor! I know because I was runnin' too.

Just as I'd turned to run, I seen bees or some damn thing, a-swarmin' out from that pipe that Dunc had blackened with his flame thrower, and I wasn't takin' no time to examine 'em because they was stingin' my ass, and everybody else's too, or everybody but cept Dunc that they seemed to be a-flyin' right over to get at us.

We all hit for the house where Wylie'd was headed, but whenever we got there, that old bugger'd went and locked the door on us, so we had to scramble for our cars, a-slappin' at them killer bees or whatever was stingin' shit out of us. I never thought I'd make it.

Soon as I dove into my pickup, I had to squish a half-dozen killers that'd followed me in, me swingin' like a damn windmill, and I realized that them dumb kids had went and plugged a pipe with a damn hornet's nest in it. The war hero's flame thrower had stirred 'em up somethin' fierce.

Well, whenever them hornets finally calmed down, we went to fetch Dunc's body. Me and Earl trotted over to where the big guy was sprawled without a damn hornet bite on him. He looked like a stunned beet. His face it was all scorched. He never had no hair left on it a-tall: no eyelashes, no eyebrows, no head-hair about halfway up his scalp and, best of all, no mustache. Us boys we glanced at each other and, hornet bites burnin' us or not, we grinned.

Since some of them suckers was still buzzin' around, we helped the big guy to his feet and hustled him to his pickup. We wasn't too keen on stickin' around there anyways. About then, Wylie come out from the house and before I could chew his ass for lockin' us out, he said, "Are them killers still here?" He was so serious that I had to laugh, bites ablaze or not.

"Naw," I said, after I quit chucklin'. "I believe Dunc got 'em."

"What's so damn funny?" Wylie demanded, but I ignored him.

Earl, that was also grinnin' despite some welts on his face from them hornets, he said, "No shit, Dunc. You done her."

"I done her," the big lunk mumbled, his bare face lookin' like a talkin' butt.

That's when Wylie piped up: "You done 'er, Dunc! You damn sure done 'er. You deserve a damn medal is what!"

Bob Don was smilin' too, but he also looked a tad worried. "We'd better run him over to the emergency room and have a doctor take a look."

Earl didn't look like he felt guilty, because he was still laughin'. "Good thing you didn't wear a mask like them chickenshit firemen do, Duncan."

Dunc never said nothin'.

"No sir," Earl went on, "no mask for Duncan. He's too smart for that."

We run Big Dunc over to the emergency room, Earl

34

sayin' that he'd give all he owned to see Dunc do it again and breakin' into laughter ever' time he thought of it. Dunc he was silent as a turd.

Well, it turned out the big guy hadn't but scorched hisself. Soon as we left the hospital, Wylie he went to carryin' on about Dunc savin' him from them killer bees, then the hero hisself took to braggin'. And the more he talked, the more he believed what he said: He'd saved Wylie's life; he'd saved Oildale from disaster; he'd saved America from a "commonist" plot! It never dawned on us guys that anybody but Duncan could take Duncan serious.

Next thing you know, he's a wounded hero, and he took to actin' like ol' Audry Murphy, and he's been at it ever since, tellin' everybody all about how he saved the world from them commonist killer bees, and he even brought that damn flame thrower of his to the Tejon Club for folks to oooh and aaah over, and what's crazy is that they done it.

Ol' Wylie's right there to back him up too. "That's it! That's the deal that it took care a them killer bees. Me and Olive ain't seen a one around the place since Dunc done the job. He's a natural hero is what! A natural hero."

When us boys begun to realize that we'd let it go too far and we was gonna blow the whistle on him, we couldn't say nothin' without folks thinkin' it was just sour grapes against the natural hero, especially since by then the liberal medias, in the person of this specimen from the *Oildale News*, even interviewed the idol, and Dunc was just as brave as could be, what with his battle wounds and all. He never said a word about the medias bein' commie rats. He did mention that he was a veteran, though, the best in his outfit at one thing or another.

So the natural hero sets there a-sloppin' down free beer, and we know we're a-gonna have to listen to him twice as bad as before and twice as long too. Sometimes it seems like you can't win for losin'. But Bob Don he's got this plan.

"Listen," he says, "let's call that guy from the *Oildale News* and see if we can't get a campaign started to send the hero off to some famous hospital for a mustache transplant. What do you guys think?"

Sounds good to me. ▣

The Great Waldorf Astoria Caper

for Don Graham

Right after Shoat Wilhite made that bundle in the Cuyama oil strike, he wheeled back to Texas in a new Caddy to impress all the home folks. And I guess he done'er, too, since he come back to Oildale sportin' a wife.

Now you folks might not be surprised to hear that, but you never seen Shoat. If ever a guy was give a true name, it was him. Hell, I seen lots of hogs better lookin' than that sucker. To begin with, he never had no nose, just this little flat nub covered with beer blossoms. He had the teensiest eyes, too, and these pointy ears. His skin was the color of a Poland China and what little hair he had was cut in a burr, so he even had these bristles a-stickin' out of his scalp. Hell of a specimen to look at, but a good ol' boy.

Shoat, hisself, he claimed his sister that give him the moniker she meant "Short," but she had too much Lubbock in her twang so it come out "Shoat." He was a squatty little sucker, that's for sure, but one look in the mirror would of told him to drop the subject.

Anyways, whenever he come back from Texas with that wife, it liked to knocked the boys off our barstools. See, we was settin' in the Tejon Club that evenin' when him and the new missus blowed in. We never knew he'd got back but we wasn't surprised to see him, 'cause even if he had hit the big money, he'd never forgot us boys that'd worked with him in the oilfield. He never acted like his shit didn't stink.

When me and Earl and Bob Don seen the woman he brung in with him, well, we was semi-stunned. Nedra, ol' Shoat's wife, she was a looker. Oh, she was all painted up with purple eyelids and lips like liver, and her hair it was lacquered. She even had false eyelashes about three inches long. But her basic equipment looked damn prime to me. While we was noddin' and shakin' hands and sayin' how pleased we was to meet her, I was thinkin' baffled would of been a better word.

On top of her looks, she told us she'd graduated the University of Texas, so her and Bob Don that graduated Bakersfield Junior College, they commenced some highfalutin' talk while me and Earl gabbed with ol' Shoat. Me, I eavesdropped and I heard her talkin' French or some such. I couldn't make out exactly what they said, then she give a big giggle and said real loud, "Carpe diem, Mistah Bundy, carpe diem."

I poked Bob Don on the ribs and whispered, "What the hell's that mean?"

He hesitated, then grinned. "Fish of the day," he explained out of the side of his mouth. He's a smart sucker, Bob Don.

Just about then Shoat told us that Nedra'd been third runner-up in the Miss Texas contest a few, quite a few is my guess, years back, and she just kind of give us a Shirley Temple imitation — shakin' her curls and puckerin' them lips — whenever he told us that. She had one hell of a set of knockers, I'll say that much, but she was a little long in the tooth to be actin' so damn cute, her drippin' them "y'alls" and "sho'nuffs" like a jug leakin' syrup.

I, at least, was beginnin' to get the feelin' she was lookin' down her nose at us. It was just somethin' in how she acted, like she was a-doin' us a favor to even talk to us. Still, we might of jawed real sociable with the newly-weds all evenin' if Big Dunc hadn't showed up. Now him and Shoat had never got along real good. They just sort of tolerated each other because the rest of us was pals. The big guy just nodded and set and ordered him a beer.

Shoat and Nedra was sweet-talkin' the hell out of each other, him callin' her "Hon" and "Babe," her callin' him "Dahlin'" and "Sugah Plum." He looked more like a porker than any plum to me, but us boys never said nothin'. Ol' Shoat he was eatin' it up, grinnin' like a coyote chewin' stink bugs.

Dunc, meanwhile, he was sloppin' his second beer down. He ordered a refill, then growled, "Ain't you two got no *names?*" Dunc never took no Dale Carnegie course, or if he did he flunked.

Shoat, that he wasn't afraid of nobody, he felt obliged to defend the family honor, so he sidearmed a giant dill pickle plucked from the jar on the counter and it smacked the big guy square between the eyes, the juice semi-blindin' him. Dunc reared up and took one hell of a poke at Shoat, but he misfired and knocked the third runner-up for Miss Texas damn near out of her girdle, poppin' her false eyelashes clean off and lopsidin' her boobs.

Me and Bob Don and Earl we jumped between Shoat and Dunc, so the new groom he took to helpin' his ol' lady out the door, him lookin' madder'n a broke-legged centerpede, her lookin' like the centerpede itself. I figured Shoat'd be back to settle with Dunc directly, 'cause ol' Shoat'll fight till hell freezes over and a round or two

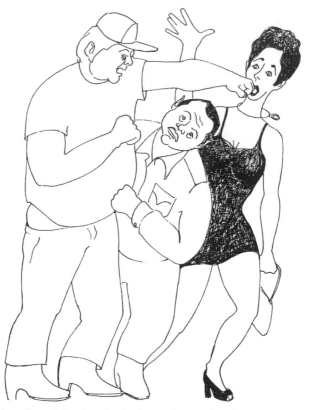

on the ice, but his dearly beloved was lookin' more like his dearly departed, so he give her all his attention.

A minute or two after he hefted Miss Texas out the door, her head popped back into the club and she screeched at Dunc, "You'll be hearin' from mah attorney! Ah'll be seein' you in cou't!" Her voice it'd lost all its cute little girl ring.

Then Shoat's gourd thrust through the door and he said, "I'll just plain be seein' ya," and all us boys knew he meant it. Dunc never seemed too impressed. The big man was a-wipin' his face with a bar towel and he shot right back, "If you're still here whenever I get my eyes clear, you ain't a-gonna see shit!"

40

Shoat jumped through the door and made for Dunc, but me and Earl and Bob Don got between 'em again and run Shoat off. As it turned out, it was a good thing we did, 'cause that ol' gal did have a lawyer, and Dunc never needed no more trouble than he'd already made for hisself.

Next day, this cop showed up at the Tejon Club and he advised Dunc that if he never apologized, he'd go to the slammer sure as hell. Dunc had to do her, too. I mean, how can a workin' stiff hire hisself a mouthpiece and fight somethin' like that. But I'm not sure Dunc got the worst of it when all's said and done.

His wife callin' the cops and sickin' that shyster onto Dunc really humiliated ol' Shoat that was used to settlin' matters more directly. He laid low for a long time. When I seen him at Woody's Liquors a week or so later, he told me he couldn't even fight Dunc now that Nedra'd went and got the law involved 'cause they'd both have to be worried about what his ol' lady might pull. He felt like Dunc'd whupped him by default.

Ol' Dunc he was pissed, too, but more'n that, he was shocked. Damn, he was always beefin' guys, and nobody never called no law on him before. It just wasn't fair. It was like somebody went and changed the rules without tellin' him. He, naturally, wanted to take it out on Shoat: "I'll stomp that ugly little peckerhead whenever I get a-holt to him," he snarled.

"Hey," advised Bob Don, "you can't even talk that way anymore."

"Says who?" demanded the big guy.

"The danged judge is who. Don't you remember you're on a restraining order?"

"I always talk thataway," Big Dunc asserted.

"Not now you don't," warned Bob Don that kind of liked to be the expert on stuff, "not if you don't want to vacation at the county road camp."

"Shit!" Dunc spit on the floor. "The damn lawyers and judges and do-gooders have took over, see! Gimme another beer, Earl." He set there for a minute, then he added: "Can't even kick a man's ass when you want to. Whatever happened to the damned Bill a Rights?"

Wasn't none of us could answer that.

Right up the street from the Tejon Club, ol' Shoat kept this little hole-in-the-wall office. He never had nothin' but a telephone, a file cabinet and a bookkeeper. He hung out there most days, and come slippin' down to the club ever once and awhile to wet his whistle. All that stopped after he brung her nibs back from Texas.

His wife she hired this fairy to come and decorate the office with fancy rugs and curtains and pictures on the walls. She hired a secretary to answer the phone, too, and she leased half-a-dozen more rooms, which that gay deal also painted up. On the front window she had wrote in big huge gold letters, WILHITE ENTERPRISES. Right underneath, in letters almost as big, it said: NEDRA MARIE DUBARRY WILHITE & ARDIS DON WILHITE, PROPT.'S.

Whenever Bob Don seen her name come first, he just winked. Wylie Hillis, this ol' fart that hangs out at the club, he said, "I believe this is one a them deals where a guy's pecker got him in real trouble." He nodded his head, then added, "The thangs a guy'll do fer nooky."

That ex-beauty queen she sure knew how to spend money if she never knew nothin' else. Before long she's drivin' to and from the country club in her own Caddy convertible and she's chummy with all these rich folks. The only Country Club Shoat cared about was malt liquor that come in cans.

More'n that, she was buildin' a damn umpire is what she was buildin'. First, she bought the trailer court over by Kern River, then a liquor store by Standard School, and that feedlot out by the Golden Bear Refinery. Directly,

42

she brung in this other ol' boy from Texas to be her "manager," a young, good-lookin' kid that wore these fancy suits, and I believe was a-gettin' in her pants. Shoat never seemed too happy about none a that.

The first time I ever seen the third runner-up all chummy with that young stud, I wondered if maybe he wasn't her son, then one day I seen 'em neckin' in her Cad where it was parked behind the office. Well, I knew then they wasn't no mother and son. They'd looked semi-hot is how they'd looked. Directly, she went and bought that kid a Caddy of his own. I never said nothin' to Shoat about what I seen, but I could tell he was takin' the whole business — her phony country club ways, her damn umpire, her fancy man — damn hard. He was gettin' plenty sore, but I believe ol' Wylie'd called it right: That gal had Shoat where he lived.

Long about then this article come out in the *Bakersfield Californian* newspaper that said Nedra Marie Dubarry Wilhite was a "daughter of the old Confederacy, a beauty queen in her native Texas, and an honors graduate of the state university." A little further on it said, "This combination of beauty and brains is a dynamic new force in Kern County's business community." It also said she'd been "a well-known chanteuse in her native state at the time she met Kern County businessman Ardis Don Wilhite."

I was readin' that article aloud to the boys, so I stopped and asked, "What the hell's a `chanteuse'?"

Big Dunc that was slurpin' a beer he grunted, "It means `shack-job' in Mescan, see."

Bob Don he chuckled. "That's a French word for dancer," he explained. I tell you, he's a real smart sucker that Bob Don, but Dunc give him a sour look.

The followin' Monday a billboard appeared on the big ol' vacant lot next to the Tejon Club where us guys parked. "Future-Home of the *Oildale Waldorf Astoria,*" it said in these green letters, then in smaller black print was wrote:

100 Rooms
Gourmet Restaurant
Olympic Pool
Two Cocktail Lounges
Ballroom
Convention Center

Under that, in red: "The Finest Hotel West of the Mississippi." At the very top of the sign, in bright orange, was the biggest letters of all: "*NEDRA MARIE DUBARRY WILHITE PRESENTS.*"

"Looks like she finally nudged Shoat clear out of the picture," observed Bob Don.

Ol' Wylie Hillis he said, "Seems like this is one a them deals where the guy makes the money, and a gal makes him."

"Them's some expensive knockers," I agreed.

A day later "No Parking" signs showed up on the lot, and later wooden stakes with colored plastic strips commenced growin' there like wildflowers. A couple guys with bulldozers begun scrapin' and levelin' the lot, and Earl that run the Tejon Club he told us flat out that ol' Nedra'd vowed to put him out of business and that her project was already a-hurtin' him. Wasn't none of us had seen Shoat for a long time.

It was about then that Bob Don come up with the plan. He busted in the door of the club and he asked — smirkin' like a hound that found the cat box — "How'd you boys like to help our neighbor Mrs. Wilhite erect her new hotel?"

"Huh?" we all said. We never wanted to help Miz Wilhite do nothin' but cept go back where she come from.

Still grinnin', Bob Don explained: "You guys remember that sorry ol' outhouse of Spud Harmon's? It's
been years since he got his plumbing, but he's left the old
shitter up for black widows to breed in."

"So what?" growled Dunc that couldn't blow his
hat off if his brains was nitro.

Me, I caught on right on. "We're a-gonna borrow
that sucker and haul it onto Nedra Marie's lot, right?"

"Right!" snapped Bob Don, "except we've already
borrowed it. It's at my place. Let's go paint `Waldorf
Astoria' on it, then sneak it onto the queen's lot."

That was just what we done, but cept that I thought
up one slight addition: This ol' boy named Bo Simmons
that used to work in the oil patch he run a taxidermy business out of his garage and somehow he'd picked up that
moth-eaten stuffed kangaroo that looked like it come to
America to get its acne cured. Well, we swung by Bo's
and I told him what we had in mind, and he loaned it to us.

After we'd painted "Waldorf Astoria" over the
shitter's door and "N. Wilhite, Propt.'" under the half-
moon, we snapped this ol' brassiere — one that Earl's top-
heavy wife had throwed away — onto the kangaroo, then
stuffed the cups with newspapers. We set it on the glory
hole, the mangy animal lookin' semi-dazed, like maybe
it'd been waitin' to use a outhouse for quite a spell. After
inspectin' the whole shebang, I painted one more sign and
hung it around the critter's neck. It said, "Miss Texas, 3rd."
While the rest of us was workin' on that decrepit kangaroo —suckin' down a few suds to stay loose — Big Dunc
that had been actin' strange, which wasn't all that strange
for him, he snuck off by hisself and made this other little
sign he wouldn't show none of us. We're curious, but we
got to laughin' so hard at the big-boobed kangaroo a-settin'
there so prim that we flat forgot about him.

Whenever we finally made it to the lot, we un-
loaded the Waldorf right in front of the sign, then Bob Don

and Earl they climbed up and crossed out "Future Home of." "That oughta fix her," grinned Bob Don, and Earl that was still up on the sign he slipped and liked to busted his damn neck. While we're a-puttin' him back together, helpin' him over to the club for a few medicinal spirits, this other idea it hit me, so I hustled three broke-down ol' chairs and a spittoon from the card room, then set 'em up in front of the shitter along with this other sign I made with a markin' pen and a tore-off cigarette carton, "Lobby."

What I never noticed was that Dunc had snuck his own sign onto the outhouse door after I finished fixin' up the lobby. Next mornin' when I drove by, there was already a big crowd and the grown-ups, at least, seemed like they appreciated Dunc's addition, but I never. "Shoats Best Erecshun" put the blame on the wrong Wilhite, so I jerked the damn sign down.

Didn't none of us but Earl see ol' Nedra Marie, us havin' to work, but he give us a rundown on what happened. Seems that her nibs showed up with her mouthpiece and her manager, and it was none other than the third runner-up that pussyfooted through the lobby and unlatched the shitter's door. Earl said the big-boobed critter — the kangaroo, I mean — it kind of leaned forward, nodded almost, as if to say, "Howdy, pleased to meet ya. I'm just finished myself. Come right in and use the facility."

Earl claimed that ol' Nedra Marie Dubarry Wilhite liked to used the facility in her britches she was so scared. She let out a war-whoop and jumped, he claimed, then clutched her blow-dried fancy man that knew just what to do, helpin' the poor, faintified thing back to her Caddy. They burned off, the whole bunch of 'em, and Earl said the kangaroo just kept leanin' from the door — one tit in, one tit out — like it's watchin' 'em leave. It done ever'thing but wave so-long, or so Earl claimed. I'd give a week's wages to've seen it.

As usual, it never took ol' Nedra's lawyer no time to get to work. Before lunch that same cop that had dealt with Dunc before, he assembled us guys at the Tejon Club. I think he liked the joke near as much as we did, but he had a job to do. We never blamed him. "Well, boys," he said, "you've really done it this time. You've got the power of Wilhite Enterprises after you."

"Shoat too?" I asked.

"We haven't heard from Mr. Wilhite," he acknowledged, then he went on: The Chief told me to tell you that if the offensive material isn't removed by 2 p.m., criminal charges will be filed. You also have to apologize and clean up the sign you defaced."

"We never done it, see," claimed Dunc.

"Shut your face, Duncan," warned the cop. "Well, boys?" he said to us.

"We'll move it," Bob Don replied. "And we'll fix the sign."

"Good," smiled the cop. "You can make arrangements with Mrs. Wilhite's manager about the apology. She still might sue you for humiliating her, though," He paused then winked. "You boys did a darn good job of that."

"Thanks," Bob Don said.

The cop smiled and nodded. Soon as he took off, I said to Bob Don, "That cop never give us no route to follow, right?"

"Yeah."

"Then let's make a grand tour of Oildale out of it, tour ever' damn street in town on our way out to Spud's." That's just what we done, too, with all us boys, cept for Bob Don that was drivin', settin' in the bed of the pickup with the shitter and the kangaroo, a-wavin' at folks and clenchin' our hands over our heads like we just won a championship, folks cheerin' and laughin' like it was the damn Rose Bowl parade. That kangaroo it looked real proud.

Not two weeks later a story broke in the newspaper that Shoat's bookkeeper had discovered that the third runner-up for Miss Texas and her boyfriend was dippin' into the till. Turns out, Shoat'd had his bookkeeper checkin' on them two right from the start. There was some complicated stuff in it, but the upshot was that Shoat run 'em off. One day they was here, the next they was gone...that fast. I heard he told 'em they could choose Texas or jail. And the third runner-up she had to agree to one of them annulment deals.

Before another week had passed, that hotel sign was gone; the shyster'd disappeared too; all that gold paint was scraped off Shoat's window, and he'd give them two spare Cads to the bookkeeper and the secretary. He also give the bookkeeper a raise, or so I heard. Then Shoat come back to the Tejon Club.

"Looky here, it's ol' sugar plum, see," growled Dunc that seen him first. He was semi-tight.

Shoat ignored him and walked up to the bar. "Boys," he announced, "go back to parkin' where you want. The Waldorf is closed."

I slapped him on the back. "Have a beer, Shoat," I said, real happy to see him again.

Thanks, Jerry Bill," he smiled. "I'll join you for a brew d'rectly. But first I wanta know who put that one sign up on the outhouse."

For a minute nobody said nothin', then Dunc he grinned real evil. "Which sign'uz that, see?" he asked, a-winkin' at Earl.

Ever'thing went quiet for a minute, and Shoat he just glared at the big lug. Then Big Dunc commenced gigglin', "He-he-he!"

He was still gigglin' whenever that giant dill pickle flew down the bar like one of them international ballistical missiles and — splat! — popped him right on the forehead. He come off his barstool a-wipin' his eyes, but Shoat's on him like a boar on a gopher snake. Dunc never knew what hit him. ▤

49

The Great Riverview Shivaree

If she'd of went to college, ol' Bob Don's latest honey coulda majored in ugly: A-plus. What the hell he seen in her I'll never know, what with him bein' a smart sucker, a educated man and all, but I guess it ain't brains does your thinkin' when it comes to women. This gal she was built like a avocado.

Not that Bob Don hisself was any great shakes. In fact, he wasn't built a whole lot better'n her — different, not better. Him, he was one of them skinny guys with a beer belly, assembled like a toothpick with a cocktail olive in the middle, or maybe a snake that et a watermelon. He looked like the "before" picture in a damn Charles Atlas ad.

Anyways, him and his avocado they come slidin' into the Tejon Club together that first time to have 'em a little libation before a-hittin' Lorene's Cafe for the special. "Two beers," Bob Don ordered.

Earl that owned the joint he walked right by me and Dunc to draw two drafts and he whispered out the side of his mouth as he passed: "I wonder if she laps it out of a bowl or just drinks it?"

They finished their beers and got up to leave, so I sung out real loud, "Congratulations on gettin' that clap cleared up at the clinic, Bob Don." The boys all laughed.

"Clap?" said the avocado and Bundy he give me the evil eye.

After them two lovebirds had left, I said to Earl, "Where the hell does Bundy scrape 'em up? He takes out the worst-lookin' women I ever seen."

"Yeah, he does," agreed Earl, squirtin' tobacco juice in the general direction of a spittoon, and adjustin' his toothpick.

Big Dunc cleared his throat and pronounced real solemn: "It's gotta be something wrong with a guy that'll love up somethin' like that, see. Too much school I b'lieve. Clouded his eyes readin' all them damn books, see."

Dunc, that had nice clear eyes on account of never even ownin' a library card in his life, he was jealous because Bob Don'd graduated Bakersfield Junior College and worked in a office. I never brought that up because Dunc he had fists about the size of a pork shoulder and if you was close to him like I was, he could use 'em too.

"I reckon Bob Don just figgers nooky's nooky. Period," said Wylie Hillis that he was settin' at the other end of the bar. We was still half pissed at the ol' Arkie for trickin' us.

"That's what I always say," agreed Earl, that's not no threat to ol' Rudolph Valentino. In fact, he was more a threat to Rudolph the Red-Nosed Reindeer that he favors.

"Well," added Big Dunc, "he looked real took with this latest 4-H Club reject, see."

It's true, he did. But that was nothin' new. He liked big gals and he'd brung some of the durndest flowers I ever seen into the club, like that one frizzy redhead that she wore a leather vest, rode a motorcycle and had this big anchor tattooed on her shoulder; she looked like ol' Blutto to me. There was that heavy lady that she went to the Church of Christ; that one got Bob Don on the wagon and give all of us hell for drinkin' beer. Finally ol' Duncan he'd got fed up and said, "There's about to be a ass-kickin' contest in here, lady, and you'll be providin' the ass, see." She took off with Bob Don chasin' after her.

My favorite, though, was that great big Indian gal he sported for a couple months. She was half-a-head taller'n Bob Don and whenever they danced, it was nose-to-tit — he loved it. He stayed all starry-eyed till she got drunk one night and knocked the piss out of him. I tell ya another thing about that gal, she could really burp: She liked to broke the Tejon Club's windows with some of them roarers of hers.

Despite all the to-do, none of us boys really figgered Bob Don's romance with the avocado would amount to much. But he kept bringin' her around the club, and purty soon that sucker's spendin' more time with her than with us. Ol' Wylie, he sidled in one evenin' and asked, "Where's the damn perfesser a-keepin' hisself? Ain't seen hide nor hair a him for a spell."

"Him and his lady friend're out," I said.

"Gettin' purty thick, ain't they?"

"She's real thick, see," grunted Big Dunc, that's purty damn thick hisself. He was all hunched over a beer with his crack squintin' like it was standin' guard for a rear attack.

"Reckon they're a-gonna git hitched?" asked the ol' Arkie.

"That's Bob Don's bidnis," I answered, but I had the same question myownself.

"They need a ox-yoke to hitch _her_, see," observed Duncan, just witty as hell that day.

Maybe it wasn't none of my business, but I was concerned that maybe Bob Don *would* be tyin' the damn knot. Don't ask me why, but he was the last bachelor in our group of guys that'd knew each other since high school. He was the one who always come up with the best ideas, the best tricks. We'd had us some high ol' times till this gal come along, but now he was spendin' all his time with ol' what's-her-face, Skeeter. What the hell kind of name is that for a gal the size of a cotton bale?

As it turned out, Ol' Wylie he was right. Not a month after that conversation with Hillis, Bob Don he slipped into the club one afternoon and announced real proud, "Shake my hand, fellas. Skeeter and I just got back from Las Vegas. We're married."

For a second none of us said nothin' because we was semi-stunned. Then Dunc, that was married to a cute little trick named Dee Dee, he upped and said, "Well, if I had'er to do over again, see, I'd stay single. Thinka all the strange stuff I could get."

"Anything you could get'd have to be strange," I said.

Duncan put down his beer and narrowed his eyes at me: "You're a-fuckin' with yer pulse, see."

Bob Don he ignored our exchange, and said, "Anyway, I just want you all to be the first to know. We're living over at my place. You're all welcome to drop by for a visit. I've got to run," he said, "Skeeter's waiting dinner," and off he went.

"Well," said Earl as soon as the new groom had left, "He really went and done'er."

"Yessir, he did," agreed Dunc.

There we set for awhile, me feelin' a tad troubled. Havin' the last of the gang hitched changed everything. I never even noticed ol' Wylie Hillis slip in the door and climb onto a stool way down at the end of the bar, that unlit corncob pipe in his mouth. After a minute or two, though, I heard him say to Earl, " Just hitched ya say?"

"Damn straight."

"Well..." he spread his spotted ol' hands like a preacher, "aren't you boys gonna give him and the new missus a good, ol'-fashioned shivaree?"

I looked at Dunc. Dunc looked at me. We both looked at Earl. He looked back. Finally, Earl he said, "Why not? That's a good idea. A damn good idea...," he hesitated, "...of course, it wouldn't *cost* much would it?"

Duncan he grinned. "Yeah, that sounds like fun. Let's do it, see."

Well, the damage had been did, so we might as well have some fun; I nodded too: "Okay, I'm in on it."

"Y'all better hustle yer bustles, then," ol' Wylie he enthused. "Let's do'er right away while they're still newlyweds. I'll call the missus and get her to cook up some grub. You boys can call yer ol' ladies and do the same. Let's git to crackin'!"

"Our ol' ladies!" we said in unison.

"I ain't callin' *my* ol' lady, see! asserted Big Dunc. "How come us to bring the War Department in on it?"

Wylie wasn't discouraged. "Hell yeah! Shivarees is family deals."

"Families!" howled Duncan. He had the damndest bunch of kids you ever seen is how come him to complain. They was livin' proof ol' what's-his-name, Darwin, he was right.

The ol' Arkie he was real took with the notion. He smacked his lips and asked, "Are we or ain't we? What's wrong with you boys, anyways?"

"Okay, I nodded. "Like I already said, count on me and Heddy."

"Sure, let's do it," agreed Earl, so we decided to meet at the Tejon Club at six, then caravan over to Bob Don and Skeeter's love nest.

Truth is, the more I thought about it, the better the whole notion *did* sound. The ol' Arkie had him a good idea. I called this guy named Bo Sims that used to work with us in the oilfields and that had opened him a taxidermy shop, then I swung by Shoat Wilhite's place and told him too. Shoat he'd made a bundle in the local oil business but he was a good ol' boy. For whatever reason, he'd also bought a stuffed kangaroo off'n Bo, and he once-in-awhile drove with it in the front seat of his Caddy. It looked better'n some of the gals I'd seen Bob Don with.

The gang of us assembled just like we agreed, whole carloads with kids and all, then we motored on over to Bob Don's hacienda in Riverview. It'd been sprinklin' off-and-on all day but just then the sun it busted through, and I turned to my wife Heddy and said, "It's sure turned nice, eh Babe?"

"Yes," she said, "we'll have a fine night with beautiful stars I'll bet." She talks funny like that on account of she's a prune-picker and a school teacher to boot. But a great gal.

Anyways, we parked a block from Bob Don's that it was right next to the Kern River's levee, and we waited for the sky to turn dark. I'd called all his neighbors to warn 'em 'bout the noise, and some of them folks they was fixin' to join us. Wylie he was just bustin' his buttons...or his zipper...to get started; he'd even went and put on clean coveralls for the occasion. And he'd brung a washtub and a big ol' club to beat on it with. Me, I'd brung a cowbell and so did Dunc. Earl had his shotgun and Shoat he'd brung a bugle. All the younguns had rattles and bells and whatnots. Bo, that'd did some blastin' work years before, he disappeared over the levee with a stick of dynamite. Most of the gals they just chuckled about all of us bein' big kids.

Once things was blacker'n a stinkbug's butt, we eased our cars up to the love nest and crept out real quiet.

We got all our noisemakers out and gathered around the one window that had a light on — it just happened to be the bedroom, I knew. Wylie he raised his club and said, "Own three: one, two..."

"WHOMP!" come the explosion and kids tumbled like ten pins. I was knocked clean up against the wall and Wylie fell in his damn washtub, a-spittin' and a-sputterin'.

"Ho-ly shit!" I said, my ears ringin'. "I hope the neighbors don't call the cops."

Out of the house flew Bob Don, one leg in his Levis, the other bare just like the rest of him. He seen us and hopped right back inside, almost bowlin' over his wife — she was buck naked too — in the process.

Big Dunc that was swayin' a little and pokin' one ear, he commenced clatterin' his cowbell and hollered, "Come on you guys! Shivareeeee! Shivareeeee!"

Me, I'd dropped my bell and had to find the damn thing, then I rang that sucker for all it was worth. Earl he put his shotgun away; I guess he figgered ol' Bo's dynamite went and trumped him. Whenever Wylie finally got hisself untangled, he give that washtub hell, and the ladies they got kids put back together, although some of the little ones was scared and bawlin', so they probably helped raise the sound level. "Shivaree!" we all hollered. "Shivaree!"

My boy Craig he was rubbin' his ears. "That was *radical!*" he said, then grinned.

A minute later, Bob Don come back out from the door, his britches hitched, a shirt on, and he said, "Okay, come on in."

Well, it never took us no time to break open the bottles and start some music on the avocado's Victrola. Me, I'd brung Bob Don, that usual never drank no hard stuff, a bottle a Four Roses, and I said whenever I give it to him, "We ain't goin' home till you killed 'er, pard'."

Bein' a good sport, he took a long pull, grimaced, then tried to pass it around. "No ya don't," I said. "We got our own. That there's for the new husband."

"Thanks," and he made a face.

Wylie was already dancin' with the avocado and he pinned a dollar on her blouse the ol'-fashioned way, which we all done every time we danced with her.

"Say, J.B.," Shoat said to me, "Bo ain't come back. We better go see what's left of him. We might could put him back together."

I was still laughin' whenever the front door popped open and there stood Bo hisself, lookin' like he was a-wearin' camouflage. "That damn mud's so thick out there, I never thought I'd make it back," he said. The explosion had covered him with it, so he took a shower while the rest of us et, drank, and cut a rug.

Wylie he announced, once Bo come out from the bathroom, "All right, Bob Don, it's time to get this deal on the road. We're a-gonna take your bride and you gotta come out and find her if'n you want to bed down tonight."

Bob Don, that already wasn't feelin' no pain, he grinned and pulled on his boots. Meanwhile, Wylie, Earl and Big Dunc, they escorted ol' Skeeter — her gigglin' — out the front door and disappeared over the levee with her. Bob Don waited a minute, then he stood up and said, "Here I go."

"Wait a minute, pard'," said Shoat. "We shouldn't oughta send poor Bundy out there all alone, what with all the gators and African frogs and such in the river." He exchanged a wink with Wylie. He traipsed outside with the new groom and pulled that moth-eaten kangaroo out from his Caddy and give it to Bob Don. "You take Waltzin' Matilda with you, and no flashlight. That fifth a Four Roses'll do for a light."

So over the levee trudged the pride of Bakersfield Junior College totin' the kangaroo, while the rest of us we cheered. We went back inside just as Wylie, Earl, and Duncan slipped in the back door with the blushin' bride, and we all took to dancin' again.

Purty soon there come a knock on the front door and I answered. It was Bob Don and Waltzin' Matilda. He swayed there a minute, then said, "I can't fin' 'er. An' I losht a boot in the dang mud. Son of a buck." That never surprised me 'cause ol' Bob Don's semi-dick-fingered when he's sober, let alone drunk. He can't hardly tie a damn knot. No wonder he works in a office.

"Keep lookin'," I advised. "That Four Roses'll keep you warm."

Skeeter she had her some good records and, to tell the truth, she danced real good too. I got to where I was grabbin' her for ever' other tune, and her blouse was papered with my money. In fact, she was a real good sport. Dunc he was dancin' with Earl's four-year-old, Juanita, her holdin' one of his legs. His frau, Dee Dee, she was on the porch breakin' up a battle between two of their boys — fists flyin' from all directions. Damn good party.

Earl he answered the door that second time. All Bob Don said was, "Shon of a buck, I losht my other danged boot." Earl give him another pair that was on the porch and off him and Matilda waltzed again. He never looked too steady.

We'd all set down to eat by the third time he knocked. I answered it, askin', "Find 'er yet?"

"Naw, J.B., but I losht my dang hat."

Later, with Wylie and Dunc that used to be mortal enemies stood there with their arms around each other's shoulders. singin' "I'll Fly Away" and "That Old Rugged Cross," tears streamin' down their cheeks, while Skeeter she played the guitar and harmonized. Heddy she said to me, "You fellows better go find Bob Don. He might've drowned out there."

That'd hadn't never occurred to me and I got worried real quick. He hadn't been back for a spell. I give Shoat a high sign and said, "Let's us go find the groom."

"Sure, " he said.

We snuck outside and made for the levee when we seen this lump sprawled against my car: Bob Don Bundy. "Hey," I called, "you okay?"

"Me?" he mushed. "Hell, yesh, but I losht that dang aminal."

Me and Shoat we looked at each other, then busted out laughin'. I stuck my paw out, the groom he grabbed it, we shook, and I pulled him to his feet. Welcome to wedded bliss," I said, and the three of us strolled back into the party. ▄

The Attack of the Great Brandy Bear

for Tom Alexander and Ken Byrum

"Hey Dad," my boy Craig he called, "wasn't it last summer they threw that big party down at the ranger station?" It took me a second to catch on, what with bein' semi-winded and all, then I said, "Yeah it was, just about a year ago, I reckon."

Earl and Bob Don and Big Dunc they never took the bait — too pooped — so Craig he give it another try. "I've never saw so many kegs of beer, and the bands..."

Bob Don he finally nibbled. "Bands, way up here in Tuolumne Meadows?" he asked.

"Yeah," grinned Craig, his braces glitterin', "they were celebrating the first time a backpack party ever made it over this trail without at least one guy getting mauled by a bear." I winked at my son that's about half-sharp for a high-school kid if I do say so myownself.

The boys they never said nothin', but I seen Big Dunc look at Earl real funny. Finally, Bob Don, that's pretty quick hisself, havin' graduated Bakersfield Junior College and all, he said with this teensy smile, "Well, at least we know the son of a buck *can* be done." Duncan and Earl they never laughed, or grinned even.

We took us a blow there under pine trees next to Cathedral Creek, a long ways from the nearest barstool, and the boys they was out of their element. Them three was greenhorns and not exactly the outdoor types. Ol' Dunc he carried a bigger pack hangin' over his belt buckle than he did on his back, and his Yukon Jack T-shirt it'd been soaked with sweat before we'd walked a hundred yards. How come us to be alongside that Sierra trail is a story itself.

See, us boys we'd been settin' around the Tejon Club back in Oildale sippin' beer one afternoon about a month before, and ol' Wylie Hillis he was broadcastin' one of his stories: "Me and Myrtle had drove up this mountain road," he said all serious, "which it was a real desolate deal. Anyways, whenever we stopped to eat sandwiches, a big gi'nt grizzly bear it come out from the woods and made for us! Let me tell ya, boys, we skedaddled!"

"Oh bullshit, Wylie," I said. "I been hikin' them Sierras for years and I never seen a bear chase no one."

"Well, you been missin' somethin', Bub," he snapped right back.

Bob Don that reads all the time, he chuckled then explained just as patient as could be, "Wylie, there aren't any grizzlies left in the Sierra Nevadas. The last one was shot at Horse Corral Meadows in 1921."

You'd think that'd shut the old coot up, but no. "Me and the missus we seen one, *Perfesssor*," he snorted. He was real jealous of Bob Don's education.

Bob Don he just shook his head.

"I heard those grizzly bears're rough," said Earl that runs the joint, toothpick on the alert.

"Well, I been backpackin' for twenty years and I never had no trouble with bears," I told him, which it was true, too. I seen plenty bruins and lost a little food, but I never had no fuss with 'em. "About the only time those bears can be a problem is if you run into a sow with cubs, then she might attack if she figgers you to be a threat. But I'm talkin' black bears, not grizzlies. Grizzlies're long gone."

"I tell ya, Dan'l Boone," sneered Wylie, that's never backpacked a step in his life, "you and yer mountain men there give'er a try this year 'cause them grizzlies're back. Me and Myrtle we *seen* one." He dipped his chin real strong, then off he walked in a huff — full of shit like always.

Anyways, that's what got me and the boys to talkin' about backpackin'. Before long, while the brew it kept flowin' purty good and our tongues got real loose, Earl and Bob Don and Big Dunc they decided that they oughta give it a try — "Shit, if Jerry Bill can do that packin' deal, *anybody* can, see," Dunc winked at the others — and we agreed to take us a week off and hit for the hills.

"Me, I always wanted to try that stuff," said Earl. "It's pretty cheap to do, ain't it?" he added.

"Count me in, see," Big Dunc chimed in. "I'uz the best hiker in my outfit back in the army." He was the best *every damn thing* back in the army, accordin' to him, anyways.

"I'm for it," agreed Bob Don.

So my boy Craig and me we planned it out, choosin' this easy trail that run from Tuolumne Meadows down to Yosemite Valley. Heddy, my wife that's a school teacher, she advised, "You'd *better* choose an easy route because you're apt to have to carry Big Drunk most of the way." She talks highfalutin' like that — and so does Craig, for that matter — but she's a hell of gal, Heddy.

"That's Big *Dunc*," I corrected.

But it turned out Heddy she was right. Here we was, just startin' out really, and Duncan already looked like he'd been shot at and missed but shit at and hit. He plopped there like a road apple next to the trail with them other two whenever Craig took to kiddin' 'em. Wasn't none of 'em lookin' too good. "What do you think, boys?" I finally called. "Time to hit that trail again?"

"Whyn't we just camp here, see," Dunc urged.

"Yeah," agreed Earl. He pulled his toothpick out like a cigarette and sort of looked at it, somethin' he done sometimes since he'd quit smokin'.

Bob Don that was takin' a long pull from his canteen, he nodded. "This is far enough for me," he said.

"We ain't come but about a mile, boys," I pointed out. "A solitary mile. At this rate we won't make Yosemite Valley before Christmas...next year. We need to put in two or three more miles — at least get to the top of this pull. It's basically all downhill from there." Not exactly true, but close.

"It'll be easier once we reach the top," Craig agreed.

"This deal couldn't *git* no harder, see," gasped Duncan.

Out the corner of his mouth, Craig he whispered to me: "I think Big Drunk is out of shape."

"That's Big *Dunc*," I corrected, then I turned to the boys. "Listen," I said, "I warned you guys not to split that six-pack this mornin' before we left."

"Hey, it's vacation, ain't it?" Earl interrupted.

"Yeah, it's vacation, but beer don't go too good with hikin'. At the rate you three're sweatin', that beer'll be gone d'rectly, and you'll take to feelin' better."

"Cain't feel no worse, see," grunted Dunc.

Two hours later we'd managed another mile or so. We was plopped next to this boggy little meadow where the trail forked to Cathedral Lakes. "This is the life," Bob Don he said in the voice of a man facin' the gallows. Earl he'd just downed a couple more aspirins and Dunc —

between gasps — he was tellin' Craig how he used to grab rattlesnakes by their tails and snap their heads off whenever he was a kid back in Texas. "Really?" said Craig, downright impressed.

Just then Bob Don let out a war whoop — "Eeek!" — and rose straight off the ground like a damn helicopter. "Snake!" he screamed. "Snake!"

"Where's it at?" I asked and Earl that was already on his feet, toothpick swallowed I think, pointed a quiverin' finger at a little dark ribbon about the size of a night crawler that's crossin' the trail beside us.

"Snap his head off, Mr. Duncan," called Craig, winkin' at me. "Mr. Duncan?"

Well, Mr. Duncan he wasn't no place to be seen. He'd cut a new trail straight up the hillside with Bob Don closin' on him. Them guys could sure motor, tired as they was. My boy he shook his head and grinned, then he picked the little garter snake up — it curlin' right away around his hand like they do — and he stroked its tiny head. Earl backed way off. "I think I'll show this to Big Drunk when he gets back," Craig said.

"That's *Dunc*," I insisted.

We finally made camp a hour or so later next to a boulder on this little flat beside another small creek. There was this big rock outcroppin' to shield us from the evenin' breeze. Craig helped the boys set up our two-man tent, which all the three of them intended to sleep in. Me and Craig we figured to roll our bags and pads out on a ground cloth.

I'd started my little gas-cartridge stove and was cookin' freeze-dried chili. I also had water boilin' over a campfire for instant soup, and I'd already went and mixed some instant butterscotch puddin' for dessert. "What's that, baby shit?" asked Earl, a beer-nut and pickled-egg gourmet. "Where's the steaks?"

Just then, from around behind the rock come Big Dunc and Bob Don. They carried four metal cups full of snow they'd gathered from a small drift just up the hill. "Time for snow cones," said Bob Don. He opened the pack he'd rented in Bakersfield and produced a quart bottle of brandy.

"Hey," I said, "I told you guys no booze up here."

"You also said we could have anything we could carry," asserted Bob Don.

"Yeah," I added, "and I'm carryin' *your* food because *you* said *your* pack was too heavy."

"Shut up and pour, see," Dunc said to Bob Don. He did, placin' my brandy next to me on a rock. I determined to just let the damn thing set there. Except that a minute later, I reached down and took me just a little sip. Then I took another'n. In fact, I emptied mine just about as fast as they did theirs, and had a couple more. It sure tasted good, and by supper time we's havin' one hell of a party, laughin' and carryin' on. Craig he come back from fishin' in the creek with four little trout and said, "I heard you guys way upstream."

I give him a slap on the back and grinned, "Wrap them trout in foil with a little butter in their bellies and we'll give these here greenhorns a treat." I was feelin' flat loose by then.

Smack! A damn snowball caught me on the neck and near made me spill my brandy. That skinny Bob Don had snuck off and filled an empty food bag with snow while we figgered he's takin' a leak, and he's on the attack. Well, we battled for a while, Craig in the big middle of it, chuggin' over to that snow drift for ammo, and the fight woulda went on longer but cept Earl caught Big Drunk in the nuts with a snow glob, and Duncan right away got pissed. We cooled him off with another brandy snow cone.

It was dark by the time we et, and I was drunker'n a dancin' cootie. Must have been the damn altitude, but that brandy helped too. After dinner ol' Craig he washed the dishes and I tied our food up in a tree just in case a hungry bruin happened by — but only managed to get it bear-nose high, about three foot off the ground, with Craig laughin' at me — then I crawled into my down bag on the ground cloth next to Craig's and commenced snorin'. The three muskrateers they somehow sardined into that teeny tent.

"HEYYYYY!" That scream it woke me right up. I heard one hell of a commotion and seen three flashlight beams pop on from where the tent was set up. "Bear! Bear! Bear!" come the voices. I was a little confused, my head it ached, and my mouth tasted like toad turds, but I followed them light beams and, sure enough, the bag of food it was gone from the tree: just the rope swingin' there.

"A grizzly went and snatched the food deal, see," I heard Dunc accuse, his voice quiverin'. "You said there *wasn't* no bears!"

"You shoulda seen 'im, a giant damn grizzly," moaned Earl.

"It was! It really was," Bob Don gasped.

"Huh," I said. "Well, it's gone now. Go to sleep. We'll look for it in the mornin'." I'd been in them mountains enough to know that a bear'll just eat what it can and throw the rest around, and that it wouldn't be comin' back, so I rolled over just as Craig snuck back into his bag.

After a second, it dawned on me: "You little devil," I whispered, "what'd you go and do?"

"I just gave your friends a thrill," he giggled.

I shook my head, laughed, then went back to sleep.

It was comin' light but the sun wasn't up yet whenever I heard Earl call: "I gotta take a leak somethin' fierce. You reckon it's safe?"

I opened my blinkers and there set them three woodsmen with their faces pressed against the mosquito net door of that little tent, eyes lookin' like pee holes in snow. I bet they'd never slept a wink since the big bear attack. Craig he was sawin' logs next to me.

"Dunc can go with you for a guard, " I answered. "No way, see," shot the big guy. "No way in hell." "Hell, he's already pissed his own pants," Earl added. I don't think he was kiddin'.

Oh well, I needed me two aspirins anyways, so I climbed outta my fart sack and got a fire started while them three little orphans they huddled there in the tent. Finally, Earl he inched out and walked two whole feet before he drained his radiator, lookin' around all the time like he's expectin' a grizzly attack. "Hey, you're splattering us," complained Bob Don.

"Tough shit," snapped Earl.

Me, I wandered around that big boulder we'd built our campfire against, and found the food where Craig'd stashed it, then come back and fixed the coffee. Truth is, I coulda used a couple beers to shut down that jackhammer in my head, then used that jackhammer to knock the skunk shit off my teeth: My mouth it wasn't exactly kissin' sweet.

"You should've seen that bear," said Bob Don that finally got courage enough up to crawl out of the tent and join me.

"Yeah," I grinned. They never did catch on that it was a trick.

We was a couple miles down the trail that mornin' after eatin', and I suggested that we shed our packs and hike up this little peak right close so they could see the view. It wasn't much of a climb at all and you could see from heck to breakfast from there. For the boys it was a tough decision: They sure as hell wanted to drop them packs — and the big clubs each one of 'em was totin' to fight off grizzlies — but they never wanted to walk uphill. They never wanted to walk a-tall. Finally, I convinced 'em and we leaned our gear against these trees and took off cross-country to that low summit.

Me and Craig we was the first ones back and, whenever we got there, our packs had been knocked all over hell and tore open. A damn bear had went and busted into 'em and got our food, spreadin' foil and plastic and chunks of this 'n' that all over, and in broad daylight too. I couldn't hardly believe it. I'd never had nothin' like that happen to me before.

Course, the bear itself wasn't nowheres to be seen. It'd did its damage and took off, so me and Craig we scouted around to pick up whatever grub we could salvage, not worryin' too much about whether the bruin had chewed it a little or not. Them's our eats, and I for one wasn't goin' hungry because of a little bear slobber.

Craig, he got our little campstove started and boiled some water for tea. We had to decide if we'd salvaged enough food to go on or if we had to head back the way we come. The boys, meanwhile, was givin' me seven kinds a hell.

"Oh no," wailed Big Dunc that by then had a club in *each* hand, "there ain't no bears in these mountains, see. Hell, ol' Wylie he'uz right on that grizzly deal." His head it was swivelin' around on alert for bears like he's watchin' a damn tennis game.

"You're one hell of a guide, J.B.," Earl said to me, toothpick agitated. "You brung us straight into bear country. Hell's bells!"

Bob Don he set there with his club on his lap and he shook his head. "It's *uncanny*," he said.

"Uncanny?" I smiled, but Bob Don wasn't tryin' to be funny.

"That we'd run into all these bears," he continued.

"I told you," smirked Craig that wasn't too worried.

"Yeah," Duncan nodded, "there's a lot more to this packin' deal than I figgered, see."

"There sure as hell is," agreed Earl.

"Well," I told 'em, "you might come up here ever' day for a year and not see another bear, so just relax. Me and Craig we come up ever' summer and this's never happened before."

After I give the boys some tea and that nice Sierra sun it warmed 'em up a tad, they calmed down. I fixed us each a cup of bear-slobber stew and nobody complained much mainly because it was that or nothin'. Big Dunc said he could sure use a beer — or a brandy — and we all laughed.

With everybody feelin' good again, I excused myself real polite and scuttled downslope into this little gulley so's I could heed nature's call, as they say. I was makin' for this big huge hemlock about a hundred foot below where our gang set. Whenever I got there, I smelled bear — like a real strong kennel — that I'd sniffed a few times before. I forgot my business and commenced lookin' around and, sure as hell, right through that tree's thick branches I seen the shape of a good-sized bruin outlined by sunlight.

I picked a different tree for my bathroom, then I climbed back up to the trail and said to Craig, "See that big hemlock down there?"

"Yeah?"

"Well, our friend the bear's takin' a little siesta under it."

"Really?" he asked, then he walked toward it and took a look for himself.

"You be careful," I cautioned him.

"Where's he goin'?" demanded Duncan.

I debated about how to answer, but finally figgered what the hell. "There's a bear snoozin' under that tree. Craig just went to take a peek."

"A *bear?*" Bob Don's voice was so high it could only be heard by a dog.

"No shit?" spit Dunc.

"No shit. Wanta go have a look."

"Hell no!"

"A bear? Where?" demanded Earl, club at the ready.

Bob Don, his voice still up there, he squeaked, "*Another* one?"

"It's *uncanny*," I said. I liked that word. Then I noticed Dunc struggle to his feet and commence hoofin' down the trail, no pack or nothin', his ass-crack exposed under his droopin' jeans.

"Where you goin'?" I called.

He never answered, so Earl and Bob Don they hollered at him too. We musta woke up that bruin 'cause just about then a black bear with two cubs she sorta lurched out from the cover of that hemlock and stood blinkin' her little bitty eyes, them two cubs no bigger'n a minute and cute as could be. Even then Bob Don and Earl, that was strugglin' to pull their packs on, they was still with us. But whenever I asked Craig, "You reckon ol' momma there's lookin' for another snack?" and he pegged a rock at that sow to chase her off; well the boys they retreated, hot on Dunc's heels.

Funny thing is that the trail right there it turned a hairpin around the edge of the canyon, so whenever Mrs. Bear and her babies crashed away from us, they went straight across through the trees and on up the other side until they crossed that very same path — about five foot in front of Duncan. He hit the brakes hollerin', "They got us surrounded!"

Then he barreled right back, knockin' Bob Don and Earl ass over ambition, then them two tried to scramble up, wrestlin' each other to get away from that maneater — which she had long-since disappeared upslope with her babies.

Well, it took awhile, but we finally got a shiverin' Duncan to shoulder his own pack and we tippy-toed the mountaineers back down the trail to the car, me havin' to send

Craig ahead to scout and guarantee that there wasn't no ambush. My boy he figgered it's the most fun he ever had outside of Disneyland, and I enjoyed it too, I have to admit, but Earl and Bob Don and Big Drunk they looked like they might could of found somethin' that delighted them more.

They cheered whenever we reached the trailhead and our car, them three, then they conked out just about as soon as we took off for home, curled in the backseat snorin' every one. A few miles before we arrived back in Oildale, Earl he woke up and said real sleepy, "Drop me by the club, willya? I'll buy you guys a beer. Craig, you get a coke."

So we stopped at the Tejon Club and everyone piled out and hit the bar. Who was settin' there big as life but ol' Wylie Hillis, zippered overalls, unlit pipe and all. "Looky here," he called, "the campers're back. Never took you boys long, did it?"

"Naw," I smiled, "we motored right along."

"It'uz a rough deal,see," I heard Duncan growl under his breath.

"See any bears?"

Nobody answered for a minute, then Craig he said real innocent, "Yeah, just a few. We chased them away from our food, didn't we Mr. Duncan?"

Mr. Duncan, that was up to his ears in a beer mug, he snorted, "What's that? Oh yeah. Damn rights! Pegged rocks at 'em is what we done, see."

"Is that a fact?" gasped Wylie.

"Damn rights!" Big Dunc he was gettin' braver as he went along. "One of 'em she had two babies, see, but we run her off."

"Them're supposed to be real rough," pointed out Wylie.

"Not if you know how to handle those son of a bucks," Bob Don he asserted.

"Was they grizzlies?"

71

"You damn rights!" Earl told him, suckin' on a fresh toothpick and a fresh beer, too..

"I'll be go to hell," said Wylie, "and you boys run 'em off."

"We sure as hell did," Duncan nodded, then he took another long pull from his beer.

"Bring Craig here another coke on me," Mr. Duncan he told the bartender. "And that ain't all," he went on, "you shoulda seen the size a that rattlesnake I damn near grabbed and snapped the head off of."

Wylie whistled through his false teeth, "Is *that* a fact."

"Yessir," conceded Duncan, "it ain't nothin' like a campin' deal out in the fresh air, see." He ordered a fresh beer — his fourth in a hurry — already semi-shitfaced.

"Nothin' like a little hike," agreed Earl.

"Right," grinned Bob Don that was lookin' a little tight hisself.

Craig, that was settin' next to me, he whispered, "They really had fun, didn't they Dad? Especially Big Drunk."

"Big Drunk's the best outdoorsman in the world as long as he's settin' on that barstool," I whispered back. "I reckon we oughta head for home before he commences wrestlin' that grizzly. We might could save the bear's life if we take right off."

Craig liked to fell off his stool laughin'.

Just as we hit the door, Big Drunk he said real jovial, "One thing, though — next time *I'm* a-tyin' the food deal up in a tree, see, so's them damn grizzlies cain't git at it, see." Earl and Bob Don they both laughed.

I just smiled and said, "I'll 'preciate all the help I can get." Then me and Craig we slid out the door and headed home. ▧

The Great Vast-ectomy Escapade

I come in the Tejon Club that afternoon and there set the boys, all but cept Bob Don anyways, havin' this real serious discussion. "Shit yeah," said Earl that runs the joint, "she had the biggest damn rack in our class. You shoulda seen 'em. Like mushmelons."

"Still, they wadn't no bigger'n ol' Mary Sue's, see," insisted Dunc. "Yessir, she sure as hell was fun to stand in front of in the cafeteria line, them big, soft jugs a-pushin' into your back. I liked to creamed my jeans ever'time she done that, see."

I believed him. Hell, Big Dunc liked to creamed his jeans everytime a gal *looked* at him, which wasn't all that often.

"And she knew it, too," Earl added.

"Hell yeah. She'uz hot for my body, see," agreed Big Dunc that had a lot of body to be hot for, most of it lard, and that was famous for not gettin' laid in high school.

Half the band was diddlin' this one galfriend of his, but he was stuck playin' pocket pool.

Bob Don come in about then, draggin' his anchor a bit it looked like to me, and he ordered hisself a brew. I knowed somethin' was wrong because he never said nothin' a-tall, no jokes even, just set there drawin' the outline of boobs in the sweat on his beer glass while us guys we kept on bullshittin'.

Wylie Hillis he piped up, "Why is it so many gals with big tits're so damn ugly?"

That was a real good question, and we all took to thinkin' on it and, after Bob Don, that graduated Bakersfield Junior College, he never spoke up, I said, "Hell, that's nature's way to sorta even things out. A purty face don't *need* no big boobs."

Wylie he nodded real thoughtful.

"Just look at Dunc," I went on. "He's got that big ol' body and no plumbin' to speak of. Me, half his size, and they call me tripod."

It went clean over Dunc's head. "Huh?" he said, but the boys was laughin' to beat hell.

After we quieted down some, ol' Earl he asked, "Y'all remember Mary Sue's big sister, Jennie?"

"Jennie!" gasped Dunc. "You talkin' *serious* ugly now, see!"

That's when Bob Don finally spoke up, soundin' grouchy. "Can't you guys talk about anything but women?" he said. "That's all I ever hear around here anymore."

I started to tease him some, since he usually does his fair share of jawin' when it comes to gals, but before I could Earl responded real indignant: "Why, hell yeah! We was talkin' politics just a while back, 'member Dunc? You was sayin' how much you'd like to get in that lady senator's pants?"

"You damn rights!" agreed Dunc.

Bob Don he just shook his head and never said nothin'.

"What's eatin' on your liver, *Perfesssor*," demanded Wylie, that he was jealous of Bob Don's education.

Bob Don he just smiled. Hearin' 'bout politics seemed like it cheered him up some.

"Anyways," Earl went on, lookin' at me again instead of Bob Don, "I seen ol' Jennie on the damn TV the other day, and she's a lawyer. A gen-u-ine lawyer! And she ain't fat no more. And she ain't ugly."

"It wadn't her," Big Dunc said flat out. "No way in hell, see. Ol' Jennie's prob'ly one a them circus fat lady deals nowadays, see."

"You never even seen the show," insisted Earl.

"Yeah, but I seen Jennie more'n once," Dunc snapped back.

"Well, mister smart-ass, I seen her and that lady that was interviewin' her and she said she'd graduated Bakersfield High in '54, so it had to be her."

"And she ain't fat or ugly? Be damned," said Dunc, a-blinkin' his eyes.

Me, I was semi-stunned. "I'll be go to hell," I said. "And you say she never looked too bad?"

"Looked like good nooky to me."

"And a damned lawyer to boot?"

"Damn rights."

Nobody said nothin' for a minute, then Earl he piped up: "Any of you guys ever take ol' Mary Sue out?"

None of us ever had.

"Well, I did whenever we'uz seniors." His voice it sounded downright triumphant.

"Git anything?" asked Dunc, real chummy.

"Yeah," grinned Earl. "I got the worst case a blue balls I ever had...couldn't walk for a week. Boy howdy was them suckers sore."

Well, I liked to fell off my bar stool laughin' whenever ol' Earl he added, "I had to soak 'em for a solid hour before I could go to bed." Everybody was hee-hawin' and a-slappin' the bar, everybody but cept Bob Don. That's whenever I figured somethin' had to be serious wrong, so I sidled next to him and asked, "What's wrong, pard'?"

He looked at me and I could see his face was all pale. "I gotta go in the damn hospital."

"The damn hospital," I said. "Why?"

"To get my balls carved," he said, his voice tighter'n a banjo string.

"Your *balls?*"

"Skeeter wants me to have a vasectomy."

"Your wife wants you to have one of them? How come?"

"Well," he explained, "the doc says she shouldn't have any kids, so she says it'll make life easier on her."

"Relax," advised Earl that'd been listenin', "I had me one and it wasn't nothin'."

"Nothin' to it, see," Dunc snorted.

"Me, too," I told him. "I had me one. Didn't you know that? Right after our fourth was born. Course in my case, they called it a *vast*-ectomy."

Even Bob Don laughed. Then he said, "I just don't like the idea of someone cutting on me in that area."

"Hey, that's a disaster area anyways," I said, and everybody laughed again.

"Nothin' to it, see," Big Dunc repeated.

"Me, I don't cotton none to any sawbones," Wylie Hillis told us. "Back in Arkansas where I come from don't nobody go to one. Don't need to."

"Won't nobody ever cut on you Wylie 'cause the zipper on your coveralls is rusted shut." I don't think I'd ever seen him except in that same get-up he used to wear on a drilling rig before he retired. "When's the last time you took them suckers off? You *have* took 'em off sometime, right?"

"Drop dead," he said to me, but the boys was laughin'.

I grinned. "Wylie, he don't never forget to zip his overalls, but he does forget to *un*zip 'em."

"Hell, ol' Wylie don't need no operation, see," grinned Duncan real evil. "What can't get up can't get out."

About then ol' Shoat Wilhite, that don't belong to Big Dunc's fan club, he moseyed in and give us a howdy. I filled him in on Bob Don's vast-ectomy. Things was quiet for a minute, what with so many don't-likes sittin' together and all, then Earl he volunteered, "Hell, I'll save you the money and do 'er myself, just as a favor. I got my buck knife out in the pickup. Wait a minute and I'll fetch that sucker."

"Fat chance," exhaled Bob Don. "I've seen you clean fish."

"Ain't no fish ever complained," and we laughed.

Wylie took his old straw cowboy hat off and scratched his bald dome. "What the hell is a *vast-ectomy* anyways?"

"You ever castrate a calf?" asked Dunc that don't know diddly squat.

Bob Don give him a sour look.

"Nothin' to it, see," Dunc advised.

It looked like to me Bob Don was gettin' semi-tired of all Dunc's guff, but he'd have the chance of a mouse against a bear if he took a swing at that big sucker, so I said to Wylie, a-hopin' to break the tension, "It's whenever the doc he cuts them little tubes in your sack so's you can't make no more babies."

"Cuts on you *there?*"

"Nothin' to it, see," said Dunc.

"Not me," Wylie puffed. "Nosir, not this ol' boy."

"It really ain't all that bad," said Shoat.

Wylie said he wondered did it hurt, and I said naw, but I was a little sore for a week or so after.

"Nothin' to it, see," advised Dunc.

"All of you guys've had it done?" asked Bob Don, soundin' relieved.

Me and Earl and Shoat all nodded. Wylie put his hand on his fly like he's protectin' somethin'.

Dunc said, "Nothin' to it, see."

Finally, Bob Don he said, "When did you have it done, Duncan?"

"Me? Are you shittin'? I ain't lettin' no sawbones carve on my deals!"

"Hell," I said, "they couldn't find no tools small enough to work on Dunc anyways."

"Your ass," he grunted, givin' me a hard look.

"That's because in his case there's nothin' to it," added Shoat, and Dunc he come off his bar stool with his fists semi-balled. Shoat, that'd fight a go-rilla bare handed, he hopped down and went nose-to-nose with the big guy, and us boys we right away separated 'em. Besides, Dunc wasn't too hard to pull away from Shoat. He never looked too anxious to tangle with a guy that'd swarmed him a few years back, so it didn't take much tuggin'.

That broke up the party. Dunc took off and so did Shoat. Directly, Wylie Hillis he did too, still a-clutchin' his drawers like he'd been wounded. I walked out into the parkin' lot with Bob Don that looked like he's a-feelin' better. "It really ain't that much," I assured him.

"Yeah, I guess," he grinned, "but I've never had any surgery anywhere, let alone *there,* so I'm a little wary."

"Hey," I admitted, "I'uz scared shitless, but it wasn't half bad. And Heddy she felt a lot better about things afterwards, if you get what I mean. It'uz a good move for us really."

"Thanks," he said, "that makes me feel better."

"When're you havin' it done?"

"Next week."

"Just hang loose," I advised. "Drink a few medicinal spirits in here at Dr. Earl's club and you'll be fine."

"Good deal," he grinned, then climbed into his pickup and started its engine. Just then who should swing back into the parkin' lot but Big Dunc. He come outta his truck and swaggered over to us like we was gonna have a fight, but when he got next to us he said, "That damn Shoat better watch it or I'll have to kick his stubby ass."

"Yeah," I said real dry.

"And besides, Bob Don," he added, "I been to one a them vast-ectomy oriental deals myownself, see, so that's why I know there ain't nothin' to it."

"Oriental?" I puzzled.

"Orientation?" Bob Don queried.

"Same difference," snorted Big Dunc.

"Hey!" Bob Don added real quick, "if you've been to the orientation, why haven't you had one?"

"You callin' me chicken?" growled the big man.

"I'm asking why."

I chimed in: "Yeah, Dunc, why?"

"Listen here, Bob Don, if a squirrelly little peckerhead like you gets one, see, I sure as hell will. I'll march down there the minute you get yours, see."

"Guaranteed?" I said.

"You callin' me a liar now?"

Ol' Dunc he was really on edge, so I just said, "Nope. But we'll be checkin' with ya."

That whole next week, Dunc kept carryin' on in front of ever'body, insistin' there wasn't nothin' to it. Between him and that damned ol' Wylie Hillis howlin' about how doctors just screw folks up, well they about undid all the good I'd did, you know, reassurin' Bob Don. He got tenser and tenser as the big day come closer, and Dunc for some reason kept the pressure on. "Yessir," he told this one drummer that come in, "take a look at Bob Don there. He's about to get neutered, see." Another time, Dunc called out whenever this colored singer with a real high voice come on a TV show we was watchin', "He sounds just like Bob Don's a-gonna, see." About the only time he shut up was when ol' Shoat come in; I guess Dunc never wanted to have to kick his ass.

Anyways, I finally got sick of Duncan's bullshit, so I called him on it. "Why don't you just butt out, Dunc?" I challenged.

"Maybe you want your butt whupped, see," he snapped right back.

"Let's go, lard ass!"

Before the big toad could roll off his bar stool, Earl spoke up: "You start any shit, Duncan, and you'll never drink another beer in this place. I've half-a-mind to part your hair with my attitude adjuster, so shut your trap or find another place to hang out." Earl sounded hot, and Dunc knew he meant what he said, so he clammed up. Besides, Dunc never had any other friends, so we had him by the short hairs. He finished his beer, then said, "I'll come back whenever you guys ain't so damn touchy, see," and he left.

And that's when I come up with the scheme. "Listen," I said, "it's time we shut that dip-shit up. He said he'd go in and have a vasectomy if you did, right?"

"Right," agreed Bob Don.

"Okay, and you're a-goin' in on Friday, right?"

"Right."

"Then on Thursday we give Duncan a little taste of his own medicine."

What made it double-good was that Thursday was Dunc's day off, so whenever I got off work that afternoon and hit the club, he'd been there a long time pourin' beer down his neck. I slipped onto the stool next to him, and said, "Well, I wonder how Bob Don's a-doin' over at the hospital?"

"This the day?" snorted Dunc real cold. He'd had his nose outta joint ever since I stood up to him.

"Yep. Fact is, it's prob'ly all done by now. He said he might drop by to have a beer on his way home."

"No shit? Well, I cain't wait to hear him talk, see," Dunc said, makin' his voice real high like a soprano's, tryin' to sound smart.

Just then in stumbled ol' Wylie Hillis. "Where's the *Perfesssor?*" he asked right away.

"Gettin' hisself nutted, see," answered Dunc.

I let it slide and Earl, that knew about the plan, he winked at me. I ordered another beer and listened to Lefty Frizzell on the juke box and waited. D'rectly, just like we planned, up drove Bob Don. Dunc he heard the diesel pickup and said, "That must be him now, see." He never sounded too chipper. I guess he was rememberin' his promise.

After a minute, the front door swang open, and in hobbled Bob Don on these crutches we'd borrowed, lookin' like the ass end a bad luck. He moaned real loud each step he took, and made a face too.

"Damn," said Dunc.

"I may not have no education," said Wylie Hillis, a-headin' for the door, lookin' like he might could lose his beer any second, "but I'm too damn smart to let any damn sawbones cut on me." Out he went.

I swung down from my stool and helped Bob Don get settled on the one next to Dunc. Immediately — I mean *right now_—* Dunc come off his seat and said, "Well, reckon I gotta ramble, see."

"Wait up," I said. "When're you a-goin' in for your operation, Dunc?"

"I got errands to run for the War Department, see," he said.

"Bob Don's did it," I pointed out. "Now it's your turn."

"I'll get around to it," he spit, soundin' semi-pissed and more than semi-scared.

"How was it, Bob Don?" asked Earl, and I could tell that Dunc wanted to hear and never wanted to at the same time. He sorta hovered there right behind where Bob Don was settin' and moanin'.

81

"Oh," said Bob Don real weak, "it was rough."

"I'll bet," Earl nodded.

"Well, that vast-ectomy deal cain't be all that rough if'n all you guys had one. It can't be too rough a-tall, see," Dunc said, a little of that fake courage a-creepin' back into his voice. "Don't make such a big deal outta it, see."

Dunc was gettin' flat brave. He climbed back onto his stool to finish the half-a-glass a beer he'd left. "I might just go and get me one d'rectly, see. Nothin' to it, anyways."

"Naw," Bob Don agreed, "nothin' to it. And they even let me keep these." He reached into his pocket and pulled out the damn *piece of resistance*, them bloody sheep balls we'd picked up at Pascal Ansolobehere's ranch that mornin', and he held them fuzzy deals out to Dunc.

The big guy timbered, a-keelin' over stool and all, hollerin' "Ho-ly shit! Get them nasty thangs away from me, see! Get them nasty devils away!" His face looked like a cue ball. He scuttled toward the door with Bob Don after him, a-holdin' them sheep nuts out and sayin', "Come on, Dunc. There's nothing to it. Let's call the doctor right now."

"No way, you crazy booger!" cried the big guy as he scrambled out the door. "No way in hell!" His pickup it spun rubber clean up to Chester Avenue a-makin' his getaway. The last thing we seen was two wide eyes a-starin' at us as he fishtailed away.

Bob Don he turned back toward me and Earl, still holdin' them sheep nuts in one hand, a big grin on his face. "Well," he said, "let's talk politics. What *was* that lady senator's name?" ▤

The Great Round Mountain Revelation

"Yer fulla shit, Bundy!" asserted Big Dunc. "Guns made Amer'ca great, see. It'uz them foundin' father deals that flat out told us to tote guns."

Ol' Bob Don he'd just went and said somethin' about controllin' the sale of automatic weapons after we seen this deal on TV about kids shootin' each other.

"Hell, if ever'body had 'em a gun wouldn't nobody get shot, see," asserted Duncan. "Damn liberals," he added.

"Besides that, God he's all for us ownin' guns," asserted Wylie Hillis, the other great expert. "Why it's right in the Bible! But your coloreds they ain't s'posed to, though," he added.

"Do you mean *people of color?*" asked Bob Don that read all this stuff about what was in and what wasn't.

"Yeah, your colored people a color."

"Anyway, where do you guys get that gun nonsense?" asked Bob Don, chucklin'.

"That's a true fact," Hillis asserted. "Why the very first things them damn commies do whenever they take over is take away a man's guns and ban monster truck rallies!"

"You damn rights," grunted Big Dunc. "It's in the damn Bible, too."

Bundy he was grinnin' when he said, "Oh yeah, that's right. It's in the same section of the Bible that endorses stock-car races and destruction derbies."

"Them, too?" Duncan slouched over a beer with half his ass smiling from his jeans while we'd been discussin' politics in the Tejon Club that afternoon and, as per usual, him and Wylie had everything all tangled up; them two could misinterpret a wet dream, I swear. Dunc he never goes to church, but he claims to be a strong Christian. He don't like all the right people — your Jews, your gay deals, your liberals, your Catholics — so I guess he figures that qualifies him.

Besides, his wife Dee Dee, lately she's been real strong in the Pentecostal Breath of Life Church. Like all of us, she done her share of drive-in movie wrestlin' before she got saved, but of a sudden she's a damn pillar in that church, and her goin' makes Dunc a semi-expert on that religion deal.

Anyways, once the Bible got into it, Duncan took to preachin'. "And besides that, it'uz your damn Catholics that brung wine into it," he asserted.

"Into what?" asked Bob Don, still grinnin'. "Destruction derby?"

"That religion deal is what, see."

"That's a fact," agreed Hillis. "The missus she brung home this deal that it tells the true facts, and it'uz yer Catholics done it!"

"So what?" asked Earl that runs the joint.

"Well...," Wylie stammered. He'd forgot the point, so Bob Don Bundy he asked him how come Jesus went and made some wine and give it out at that weddin'.

85

Earl he added, "Hell yeah, they had so damn much of the stuff they even washed in it."

That's when Big Dunc give us benefit of his wisdom. "It weren't wine, see," he said real definitive, like he's a-settlin' matters.

"Then how come it *says* wine?" I challenged right back.

"Your Catholics done that too, see, changed the Bible. It's really supposed to say `grape juice.' They done it 'cause they're all drunks, specially them priest deals, see. They're the worst. Why they even get drunk in church right durin' services, see. Arsh, most of 'em," he added. Dunc emptied his beer and called for a refill, cluckin' in outrage over drunken priests.

"Arsh?" said Bob Don Bundy.

"I believe he means Irish," I explained.

"You damn rights," added Duncan.

"You sure the Bible didn't mean to say Nehi Grape Soda?" I asked.

"Where'd you get that grape juice information?" asked Bob Don, rollin' his eyes. We all knew Duncan had never read a book in his life, let alone the entire Bible.

"I read it in this deal that the War Department give me, see. And it told how your Jews kill your little white babies right in their churches."

Bob Don shook his head. "That's malarky! I think whoever wrote that's been hitting the same `grape juice' they talk about in the Bible."

"Well, I'll tell ya one thang, *Perfesssor*," snapped Wiley triumphantly, "them're true facts. They was in this deal that Olive got give by these ladies that come to the door. You read that part 'bout the guns, Dunc?"

"You damn rights. The War Department she showed me that part too, see. God he's all for 'em."

"I hate to bother you with facts, but it *was* wine they drank," Bob Don explained. "Wine didn't spoil very fast, and in those days there wasn't any refrigeration, so it was an important food."

"Oh, it *was*, was it," huffed Wiley. "Well me and Dunc read the true facts in that deal that it was give out by them ladies. And, besides, I heard the Reverend Billy Ray Pottee on TV the other day, and he said the same damn thang!"

"Yeah," snorted Dunc, "I suppose you dog turds know more'n the Reverend Billy Ray Pottee, see." Him and Wylie, the two theologians that hardly ever agreed on nothin', they nodded at each other.

"He's a squirrely bastard, that Pottee," I said.

"He's also the one who sent out those dang tracts that Dunc and Wiley're talking about. They left one of those son of a bucks at our place too," said Bob Don.

"Ours too," added Earl.

"More bullshit than a feedlot," said Bob Don that hardly never cusses.

"You sayin' I'm full a bullshit?" demanded Big Dunc.

"*I'm* sayin' you are," I couldn't resist tellin' him. The big guy'd went to fat. If he ever needed to haul ass, he'd have to make at least three trips. He wasn't no big threat no more.

"Oh, yeah," he growled.

"Shut the hell up," said Earl that runs the joint, his tone tellin' us he was tired of Dunc and Wylie. He knew they never wanted their hair parted by his attitude adjuster. And Dunc never wanted to be kicked out either, or he'd have to go home to the War Department and explain why he smelled like a brewery. He'd probably tell her it was grape juice forced on him by Catholics.

Everything went silent for a minute, but cept for Dunc mumblin' — "Your damn Catholics" — then Earl he said, "Speakin' of Pottee, you boys read where he wants to put a hunnert-foot statue of Jesus up on Round Mountain. It'll be the biggest one in the whole world, he claims, and it'll bring `pilgrims' from all over the world to Oildale."

"Pilgrims?" said Wylie Hillis. "You mean in them pointy hats and buckles on their shoes? They'll get shot for hippies sure as hell if they show up around here. Why I seen these guys in San Francisco on TV that they was wearin' big capes and shit like that, and they looked somethin' like yer pilgrims..."

Bob Don shook his head. "He doesn't mean *those* pilgrims."

"Well, 'scuse the hell outta me, *Perfesssor*. But he *said* pilgrims, didn't he?"

"And the Bible *said* wine," popped Bob Don. Sharp as bob-wire, that guy; you get in a battle of wits with him and he'll just cut you to fish bait.

"What's in it for him?" I asked. "That Pottee don't do nothin' that don't help make him rich or famous or both." Pottee had showed up on the local scene a few years before and somehow managed to finagle himself a weekly television show on a local channel. He'd parlayed that into a daily show now, and he had one hell of a followin'. He was this good-lookin' guy with a fancy hairdo and expensive clothes and a shiny ring on each little finger. He give me a royal pain in the ass.

"To get richer and more famous, I'd guess," said Bob Don. "He's a self-serving jerk."

"You're talkin' about a preacher!" said Wiley Hillis real indignant.

"Yeah," added that religious zealot Duncan.

"Listen," Bob Don explained, "being a preacher isn't like being a doctor or a lawyer: There's no state certification. All it takes is a sign that says you're one, plus some showmanship, and some gullible people to follow you."

"Talkin' thataway's a good way to go to hell d'rectly," warned Wiley.

88

"Hey, the War Department, she's joined this five hunnert-buck deal a his that whenever she gets it paid off she's guaran-damn-teed to go straight to heaven, see. Think a that!" asserted Duncan. "I might even buy me in on that, too, see."

"That's just what I mean. Did Jesus charge anything to save people?" Bob Don asked.

"Yeah? Did he, Dunc? Wylie?" added Earl.

"Well..." That stumped Wiley.

"In fact," Earl grinned, "if you boys'll give me *four-fifty*, I'll guarantee you'll go to heaven."

"How the hell can *you* do that?" demanded Duncan.

"The same way ol' Pottee can. It's nothin' but words. Speakin' of words, young Jeffrey's comin' in after school today to help me clean up, and I don't want *nobody*" — he looked directly at Wiley Hillis — "sayin' you-know-what while he's here."

Wylie looked up. "But he *is* a colored," he said.

"A person of color," corrected Bob Don Bundy.

"A colored a color," said Hillis.

"And J.B. there *is* a paleface," pointed out Earl, noddin' at me, "but I never heard you mention it."

"Well," I said, "you're a-doin' good by givin' that youngster a after-school job, Earl... specially with you bein' such a tightwad and all." Ol' Earl he's still squeezin' the first nickel he ever made and the ol' buffalo's a-gaspin' for breath, but he'd took over payin' Jeffrey from us guys.

"Tight? Me?"

Bob Don grinned and shook his head. "We can hear you squeaking from a danged block away."

He *was* doin' good too, Earl. And Jeffrey he turned out to be a real good worker.

Directly the youngster he come in and took to sweepin' and cleanin'. He never complained the way most kids nowadays do anytime you ask them to do somethin', and he was real pleasant too.

Anyways, while young Jeffrey he was sweepin' up, Earl switched on the TV. "Here's your hero, Wylie, Dunc," he said, and, bigger'n hell, ol' Billy Ray Pottee he swerved onto the screen with his Eye-talian silk suit and pinkie rings a-glitterin'. He had tears in his eyes and he pleaded, "Oh, faith partners, faith partners, don't let me down. Pleeeeease don't let me down. God wants that statue built on Round Mountain! *God* wants it, not his humble servant Billy Ray Pottee! I am just his instrument, faith partners."

He made this grand gesture with his arm and a good ten thousand bucks of jewelry flashed — them two heavy rings, a thick gold watch on one wrist and some kind of showy bracelet with gems on the other one — then he stuck his mug right into the camera and moaned, "I'm just His humble servant, and between you and I, faith partners, God's going to call me home if you don't donate another two hundred thousand dollars for our statue, Christ of the Oilfields, and to the Billy Ray Pottee Foundation." He said that last part real fast so you couldn't hardly notice it. These little tears was a-tricklin' down his cheeks when he repeated, "God's going to *call me home.*" He paused, and nodded. "Pleeeeease don't let me down, faith partners."

"Where you reckon God's gonna call him to, Earl, Tulsa? Dallas? *Fresno?*" I asked.

"If that son of a buck'd sell some of those rocks he's wearing," Bob Don pointed out, "he wouldn't have to hit up on his 'faith partners' like a hooker."

Wylie never liked that. "You better watch yerself, *Perfesssor,*" he warned. "That there's a *man a God.*"

"That there's a man of wealth trying to get richer," said Bob Don.

"The War Department she's in on that statue deal, too, see," said Duncan.

"Then *you* are, you knucklehead," I said. "You bought him them diamonds right out a your joint bank account. Nice a you to help him out with them rings and that watch."

That stirred Duncan a tad. "Whadaya mean? I never bought him nothin', see! We're a-helpin' to build that Christ of the Oilfields deal, see, and the War Department she's set for heaven. And I'm a-gonna join too."

"Right, and when you're in the poor house ol' Pottee'll be walkin' around wearin' his damn Rolex."

"You don't know shit, see."

"Hush up, you two," ordered Earl, "the good part's comin' on." He nudged up the volume.

Ol' Billy Ray he'd took his coat off and he had on this monogrammed shirt and a damn gold necklace outside his shirt and over his tie with this big giant cross covered with diamonds or some damn thing. He set in this kind of gold throne deal with a big high back on it, and his helpers they commenced paradin' these sick folks up to him and he laid hands on em, rolled his eyes up, and shouted "Be *healed!*" and, like as not, they'd drop limper'n Wylie's pecker.

Speakin' of who, ol' Wylie he fell for it. "Cured that ol' heifer, by God!" he said, all slack-jawed. "That gal'uz took with the cancer and now she's healed."

"How do you know?" demanded Bob Don Bundy. "All you see is what I see, and what I see is some poor woman — or maybe some actress — faint."

"*Oh ye a little faith!*" pronounced Wylie.

"Hey Wylie," I grinned, "maybe Pottee can heal that zipper on your coveralls and you can finally get 'em off."

"I heard me enough a you sinners," he said, and with that he slid off his bar stool and left.

"*O ye of little sense!*" Bob Don called after him.

Well ol' Pottee he kept after it, jumpin' out of his throne and a-jerkin' this way and kinda hoppin' around and sort of dancin' between cures. He healed this paralyzed arm that all of a sudden was workin' again — then he hopped — and this cancer that he somehow jerked out of a guy's belly and dropped in a bucket one of his helpers held — then he danced — and he even erased this birthmark on a gal's face — then he jerked and talked in tongues. It was a good show and the audience was a-howlin'.

But I noticed something: "You boys notice not one hair on that bird's head has moved, no matter how much he dances and jumps and yells."

"You're right," agreed Bob Don.

Earl nodded too, sayin', "Hell, he must have enough lacquer on it to repaint the club here."

"You boys're funny as a damn crutch, see," grunted Dunc.

"Hey, you paid for that son of a buck's hairdo, too," Bob Don pointed out.

"Eat shit," said Dunc, as usual just full of snappy comebacks.

Well, that program it was about over so the camera it come up close on ol' Billy Ray's face and he said, "All you shut-ins, just place your hands on the set and I'll pray for you to cure whatever troubles you, and you can mail your faith offering to the Billy Ray Pottee Foundation," and this address it come on the screen.

"Quick, Dunc," I said, "put your jeans on the TV so ol' Billy Ray can heal 'em so they'll cover the crack in your ass!"

"Eat shit."

Finally, Pottee faced the camera one more time and commenced blubberin'. "Oh, faith partners, God *needs* your help *desperately* so I can build Christ of the Oilfields and the Billy Ray Pottee Foundation. I'm afraid he's going to call me home if you don't help. Pleeeeease, pleeeeease, pleeeeease, faith partners, help Christ and I, or I might be called home. Remember, mail your faith offerings to the Billy Ray Pottee Foundation," and that address come on the screen again. "Or you can phone in.

All major credit cards accepted," and this time a 800-number it come on the screen.

"Get on the phone, Earl," I urged, real dramatic, "we gotta save ol' Billy Ray."

"That's fuckin' close," grunted Earl. "I might *send* him home if he ever comes in here, though."

"Christ can do a whole lot better than that charlatan, when it comes to picking disciples," Bob Don snorted. He sounded real disgusted.

Just then little Jeffrey, that I'd plumb forgot about, he come up to Earl and said, "I'm finished, Mr. Tyner."

Earl grinned, and wiggled his toothpick. I believe he really liked that little guy. "Well, let's see here, Jeffrey, looks like to me you've done a real good job again. It's payday, ain't it?" And he went to the cash register, opened it, and took out a few bills, then handed 'em to the youngster.

I liked to had a heart attack, seein' him actually *give* money to someone else.

"What're you doing with all the money you're earning, Jeffrey?" asked Bob Don real pleasant.

"I give it to my momma," the boy said.

"Don't you get to keep none of it?" I asked.

"She give me an allowance."

"And what do you buy with it, lotsa candy?" asked Earl.

"Oh, I put most of it in my savings account so I can go to college some day, and I buy my school clothes, and I give some to the Kitchen."

"The Kitchen?" grunted Dunc. "What's that deal?"

Bob Don answered, "I read about it. It's that ecumenical program to feed the hungry that they run out of the Catholic church."

"*Catholics*," spit Dunc, makin' a face.

"There's some poor people they don't got places to live or anything to eat," said Jeffrey. "Momma says, they our brothers and sisters."

"Well, here," I said. "I want you to give the Kitchen this five when you make your donation."

"Yeah, here's another five," said Bob Don.

We both looked at Dunc. For a minute, he never said nothin', then he croaked, "Oh, *hell*. Here's five for the damn Kitchen, see."

The boy looked dazzled. *"Really?"* he said. "Thanks! I'll stop by on my way home." He headed for the door, but Earl's voice stopped him.

"Wait up," he said, and Jeffrey turned around. "Give 'em this here while you're at it," and he handed the boy a twenty.

"Gee, Mr. Earl...," said Jeffrey, and he stood there next to the owner for a minute, then he reached over and hugged him. "Thanks," he said, then he sprinted out the door, a grin across his face.

Earl he was red as a damn apple and his eyes looked a tad damp to me. "Little pissant," he said, then he cleared his throat and even removed his toothpick for a second.

Me, I grabbed my chest, and said, "Did Earl give away a *twenty*? A real twenty? Call ol' Billy Ray," I said. "I b'lieve I'm bein' called home."

"Tell ya what, faith partner," said Earl as he withdrew his sawed-off pool cue from underneath the bar, "I'm about to send you home with this attitude adjuster."

"Amen!" said Bob Don, and we all laughed. ▰

94

The Great Natural Gas Blowout

for Jim Work

Earl he was steamed. "That damn Myrna she went and left her golden egg, Danny Ray, at the place yesterday while her and her new squeeze, ol' Braxton, they went to the gun show," he shook his head. "Boy, is that kid ever a specimen. He never wanted to leave the TV and he damn near eat us outta house and home." Myrna she was Earl's divorced sister-in-law, and Danny Ray was her pride-and-joy by her first marriage...or her second, maybe.

"He's a cute kid, though," I winked at Bob Don when I said that, and he grinned back at me.

"Cute as a damn boil," snorted Uncle Earl. "Anyways, I finally got fed up and took the little fart out to the yard and asked him to help me with the lawn. He told me to kiss off — his mouth fulla my chips and my dip while he sassed me. He said, 'My momma's gonna buy me a gun and I'm gonna shoot you.'

"Well, that pissed me, so I told him to shut up and get the hell to rakin'.

"He just stood there and made a face, then he said, 'I don't shut up, I grow up, and when I look at you I throw up.'"

"No lie?" grinned Bob Don. "He really said that?"

"He was fixin' to say more, but I reasoned with him."

"What'd you say?" I asked.

"I said, 'You had enough?' after I paddled his little canoe around the yard a time or two. He had, and he raked the hell out of the lawn."

Bob Don he winked at me and said, "That sounds like child abuse, Earl."

The owner he snapped back, "Child abuse is to let the little squirt get in the habit a actin' that way, because somebody'll sooner or later strangle him."

We laughed, but Earl had him a point.

Down the bar missin' all this, Big Dunc and Wiley was huddled over beers talkin' chili. Duncan he claimed, of course, he was the best chili-maker in his outfit back in the army. "I'uz stationed at Fort Hood in Texas, see. Whenever they had this chili deal in town, me and some other boys, we decided to enter, see."

He paused, real dramatic, drained his draft, and said to Earl that runs the joint, "How 'bout anothern," then went back to his story: "Wellsir, me I went and caught us a mess a rattlesnakes, see — snapped the heads off them rascals is what I done — and put 'em in the chili pot." He was hunched over his beer with his jeans at half-mast as per usual, ass-crack airin' out.

"*Rattlesnakes!*," gasped Wylie. "Them're rough!"

"You damn rights. Anyways, we won the deal and got a hunnert bucks cash money, see." He nodded real official.

Just then Earl, who'd brung Dunc a fresh beer, made a face and asked, "Who shit?" As if he didn't know.

By then Wylie had his straw cowboy hat off and was wavin' it to clear the air. "You do that, Duncan ?" he gagged. "Damn, you're rotten!"

"Who *me?*" grinned the big guy evil as could be. He's the fartin'est sumbitch I ever knew.

The fumes reached me and Bob Don at the far end of the bar and we liked to puked. "Lord!" I said. "I hope you never *ate* that. I hope that's just somethin' that crawled up there and died."

"You really *are* rank," said Bob Don.

Dunc he was settin' there all alone now while the rest of us retreated to the open door for fresh air. "Hell," grinned Duncan, "that wasn't but a littleun I sneaked out, see. Hold onto yer hats." He exploded for real then and liked to knocked the mirror off the wall behind the bar. No wonder his jeans're always at half-mast: He blows 'em off.

"Look, Dunc," said Earl, "I'm gonna make you drink beer in the men's shitter from now on if you don't start warnin' us before you cut loose."

Dunc he just kept grinnin'. I believe he was the best farter in his outfit back in the army.

We all climbed back onto our barstools, but as far away from that gas bag as we could get. We let him set there in his exhaust cloud happy as a dog in a boneyard.

All of a sudden, Bob Don he snapped the *Bakersfield Californian* that he was holdin' and said, "Wait a minute. Maybe I've found the perfect place for Duncan."

"Where at," I asked, "San Quentin prison supplyin' gas for the chamber?"

"Listen to this. 'Coalinga — An unusual competition is scheduled for a saloon in this oilfield community. The Tradewinds intends to live up to its name next week when it hosts the first annual World Crepitation Contest...'"

"Crapitation?" said Wylie. "What the hell's that deal?"

"*Crepitation*," corrected Bob Don the college graduate that knows them big words. "It means to make loud noises like explosions...or maybe farts. It's a dang farting contest, Wylie."

"They cain't say 'fart' in no newspaper," huffed Wylie, the moral crusader. "It's against the dern constitution is what!"

"They never," I pointed out. "They said `crepitation'."

"They cain't say 'crapitation' neither," he insisted.

Bob Don ignored the ol' Arkie. "There's more," he said. "Get this: 'The owner of the Tradewinds, Oscar "Turk" Balik, invites entries. We'd like to see as many competitors as possible,' he said."

This time Earl he spoke right up. "Turk Balik? Hell, I used to work with ol' Turk up on Ten Section before I bought the club here. He got transferred to Coalinga. Sounds like he finally bought a place of his own. Always said he was gonna."

I knew Turk too. "Yeah, sounds like," I agreed. "I'll tell ya, I wouldn't start no trouble in *his* place. He's about the toughest guy I ever seen in the oil patch, a real mountain man."

From down the bar, Dunc finally piped up. "Oh yeah, I coulda took him, see."

"You coulda took him to jail for manslaughter after he knocked the pee-waddin' outta ya, maybe," I said. Dunc fights about as good as Wylie screws.

"Ol' Turk's tougher'n tank water," Earl agreed.

"Oh yeah...?" groused Duncan.

Bob Don snapped that newspaper then said, "I'll bet you can outfart him, anyway, Dunc. In fact, I'll bet you can outfart *anybody*," and we all laughed.

Dunc never laughed. "I coulda took him, see," he muttered.

I ignored him because this idea it'd struck me. "Hey, how about if we find out how good Duncan really is? Let's enter him in that fartin' contest at Turk's over to Coalinga. It'd give us a excuse to see ol' Turk, too."

"Great idea," said Bob Don.

Even Wylie joined in, his unlit pipe upright. "Dang rights! I'll bet ol' Duncan can blow anybody outta the dern ring!"

Earl's face it turned real grave, his toothpick droopin'. "How much you figure a deal like that might run us?"

He's the county's leadin' tightwad, I swear. "We'll all chip in," I said.

"How much each?" demanded the proprietor.

By now Dunc was grinnin' real proud. He cut loose just to celebrate. We all retreated toward the open door.

"Listen," I urged Earl, "it's a no-lose deal. Dunc's a cinch."

"Well...," the owner hesitated.

"Don't act like a damn queer," urged Dunc. "Chip in, see."

Earl reached under the bar and extracted his sawed-off pool cue. He patted one hand with it, bobbed his toothpick, and said, "You wanta repeat that, Duncan?"

Duncan was stupid, but not crazy. "I'uz only kiddin', see," he grinned.

"Stick with the other end, Dunc," I urged. "Your mouth's just gonna get you in Dutch."

Anyways, that's how it all got started. We eventually managed to talk Earl and Wylie into chippin' in, so a week later after work me and Dunc — the other guys couldn't get away — we drove my half-ton supercab over to Coalinga for the contest. "Damn, Dunc," I said about ten miles into the journey, "you're rotten."

"Just warmin' up, see."

"Save a little for the damn contest," I gasped, my head hangin' out the window like a dog's.

We finally arrived at the Tradewinds just about dark. It was this nice joint with a big, giant flashin' sign, real fancy paint job, and this bright banner draped across the front: "WORLD CREPITATION CHAMPIONSHIP — Friday."

Well, we slid inside and the joint it's even fancier in there than on the outside, real plush like them bars you see in the movies. It was real crowded too, full of guys all dressed up with plenty of whoopin' and laughin'. "Let's snag us a brew, see," suggested Dunc, but I told him we needed to check in with ol' Turk first, find out about the contest.

I looked around and never saw him, just all these scrubbed-lookin' guys with mustaches, a lot of 'em real big like weight lifters, so I asked this bartender where Turk was. He said just a minute, and picked up a little telephone without no wires. D'rectly, a door opened behind the bar and out come Turk hisself, all spiffed up in this fancy white suit, a buncha gold chains, and with a shirt unbuttoned damn near to the belly button. He was as big and hairy as ever, like a gorilla in clothes, but he was as friendly as ever too, shakin' our hands, pattin' our backs, and buyin' us beers. "So you're gonna enter the contest, eh Duncan. Well you ought to be a strong contender from what I remember," Turk laughed.

"You damn rights," nodded Big Dunc.

"How's old Earl doing?"

"Good," I said, "real good. He sends his best."

While we chatted I noticed that there was a little bandstand at the far end of the room. Chairs and a microphone had been set up and another one of them "Championship" banners was hung up behind it. There was a card table over there for sign-ups too, so I went over there and took care of that while Dunc leaned on the bar fortifyin' hisself.

Whenever I got back to him, I said, "You know, there's not one gal in here that I can see, except that great bigun over there."

Duncan just snorted, "Gals don't 'ppreciate good farts the way guys do, see. Hell, would *your* wife a come?"

"I guess not," I said. Somethin' seemed a little...odd...to me. But that bar it was really fillin' up.

Just then Turk, he come back and said to me, "Listen, J.B., one of our judges hasn't shown up. Would you mind helping me out? We've got entries from half-a-dozen towns and it would be better if at least one of the judges wasn't from around here." Turk's a good ol' boy, so I said sure, but I didn't know exactly what he wanted me to do. He explained it'd be just like those divin' deals we see sometimes on the TV — a guy'd cut loose, and we was supposed to flash these numbers between 0 and 10. "Don't take it too seriously, J.B.," he said. "We don't. This is all just for fun."

"Sure," I grinned.

A minute later Turk he called all the entries together and give 'em instructions while me and the other judges we set down in the front row. Dunc looked real confident, grinnin' and winkin' at me. Then I happened to notice one of the guys in the contest turn and give this other guy a big kiss. Dunc noticed too and his eyes bugged out.

I never said nothin'.

Wellsir, with all kindsa laughin' and kiddin', the big competition it got started, and some skinny little guy with a mustache — it seemed like ever'body but me and Dunc had mustaches — he walked to the center of the bandstand and squeezed a tight little poop out. Someone in the audience yelled, "Oh, a virgin!" and ever'body laughed to beat hell. I give that guy a 2, but by then I was more interested in what we'd got ourselves into. I believe Duncan was too, because his beady eyes had gone all loose.

The next guy was bigger'n Dunc and he cut a blue roarer; I give him a 9. The one after that, he managed a rumbler, and I give him 7. It went on until it come Big Dunc's turn and he sidled to center stage, looked at me for a long second, then made a face. Nothin' happened. He made another face but we still never heard nothin'. Finally, the third time, it sounded like when a cork pops

101

outta a bottle, that's all. That same voice from the crowd, it yelled, "You're supposed to fart, Honey, not tease us." Dunc never laughed. I give him a 1.

He never got no better as the contest went on. I believe his pucker cord was tighter'n a preacher's purse. Mine too, I'll tell ya, cause by then I seen guys holdin' hands and smoochin' and even ol' Turk hisself was doin' it.

Me and Dunc we was damn happy to get outta the Tradewinds that night. He'd taken last place and Turk awarded him this certificate for a free pizza, sayin', "Maybe that'll help our guest from Oildale begin training for next year's competition. I can assure all of you, from past experience, Duncan had an off-night."

"You wanta go get that pizza?" I asked soon as we was back in my pickup.

"Hell no!" he grunted. "Let's get the hell outta here."

Me, I never argued. For the first twenty miles, I noticed Dunc kept his eyes on the rear-view mirror. I noticed because me, I was doin' the same damn thing.

Pretty soon, though, he relaxed and begun to be Dunc again. "I b'lieve some a them boys back there'uz gay deals, see," he finally said.

"No shit?" I said, sarcastic as I could, but he missed it.

For a spell, he looked about as thoughtful as he ever does, then he snorted, "Gay deals. They're damn lucky I never whupped the whole bunch of 'em, see. Damn fairies."

"You shoulda started on Turk."

"Hell, I coulda took him easy." I slowed the car and the big guy he asked, "What do ya think yer a-doin'?"

"I'm gonna find a place to turn around. I don't wanta keep you from whuppin' Turk and maybe knockin' shit outta all them gay deals. I wouldn't wanta keep you from havin' fun."

"Are you *nuts?*" The look on his face made my night: He was gaspin'.

So, anyways, I stepped on it and headed back toward Oildale and he relaxed again. "Back in the army, I usta roll queers on weekends just to pick up spendin' money, see," he told me.

"That's real admirable," I said, but he missed my tone as per usual, so I added, "I'll be glad to turn around d'rectly and you can roll Turk and them other boys."

"Turk ain't no queer...big, stout guy like him. Only them little skinnyuns was, see."

"Why'uz he dancin' with that blond kid, then?"

Another long pause. "You don't reckon Turk's turned queer?"

"Kiss me and I'll tell ya," I replied.

Dunc's eyes got real big...for BBs, anyways...then he said, "You're shittin', right?"

I just laughed.

He cogitated for several miles, then asked, "You mean *all* them big husky oil workers that they was at the Tradewinds, they was...*gay deals?*" Then he grinned, "Nawww. Ain't possible, see."

"Wouldn't surprise me."

A mile later, he said, "Well, I coulda took 'em, see."

"Just like you won the damn fartin' contest."

"You damn rights." I think he realized what he'd just said because he hushed for a few miles. Then of a sudden, he liked to blowed the windows outta the pickup.

I was stunned by the explosion and I damn near swerved the truck off the damn road, and I real quick rolled down my window and stuck my head out. "Whew!" I gasped, "Where the hell'uz that fart back at the contest?"

I was still gaspin' whenever I remembered them number cards that I'd forgot to give back to Turk whenever me and Dunc we'd scrambled to get out of the Tradewinds. I grabbed the 10 and held it up.

Duncan he grinned real proud. ▤

The Great River-Rafting Adventure

There wasn't but five of us — me, Big Dunc, Bob Don Bundy, Wylie Hillis, and Earl that runs the joint — settin' in the Tejon Club that hot mornin' whenever Bob Don he said, "Look here," and showed us a color picture in the *Bakersfield Californian*. There was these big giant waves bustin' over a blue rubber raft and all these happy folks just a-laughin' and a-carryin' on. The headline it said, "Rafters Frolic on Kern River."

"Looky there," I said, "That deal sure looks like fun, what with the air conditioner gone haywire here in the club."

"The guy'll come fix it tomorrow," Earl said, suckin' on his soggy toothpick.

"And it might stay fixed for a whole damn week!" grunted Big Dunc. He'd took to wearin' T-shirts for some reason, and he hunched over his draft at the bar, his beer belly pullin' the back a his shirt up and outa his jeans, so a

104

tad of his pale cleavage hung out there for all the world to see. He's a semi-stylish sucker, Dunc.

"Screw you," responded Earl that never liked criticism all that much. His toothpick it stood up real defiant.

Bob Don ignored the fuss. "When I was a kid," he said, "there was a lot of water in the river right here in Oildale, so I used to take an inner tube up to Gordon's Ferry Bridge and float all the way down to the Chester Avenue Bridge. It was a real kick."

"Is that right, *Perfesssor?*" answered Ol' Wylie. Speakin' of new deals, Bob Don had took to wearin' these little shit-assed half-glasses he bought at the drug store, and damned if he didn't look like a professor at that.

"Hot as it is," I said, "I'd go for one a them raft deals myownself."

"You guys want to go up there?" asked Bob Don. "We could see what it costs and maybe make a day of it."

"Not me, boys," sung out Wylie Hillis that's chickenshit of damn near everything. "I don't get but one part a me wet on purpose."

"And that real rarely," I added, "on account of he can't unzip them permanent coveralls."

"Listen," Bob Don went on, "it says here they take folks out every day..."

"You read that with yer new horn-rim testicles?" asked Duncan with a shit-eatin' grin. He never read nothin' with or without testicles.

"It gives a local number to call," Bob Don went on, ignorin' Duncan.

"Well," I said, "I know my boy Craig he'd like to give 'er a go. How 'bout you Dunc?"

"Hell yeah," grunted the big guy. "Besides, I'uz the best one in my outfit back in the army whenever it come to that raftin' deal, see."

"I seem to recall you was handin' out shorts and T-shirts for two years in the supply room," I pointed out.

"Yeah?" he snapped. "Well I got my trainin' after basic in this engineers' outfit, Mr. Jerry Bill know-it-all."

"Right," I said. Full of shit as a Christmas goose, Duncan.

Meanwhile, ol' Earl that's always thinkin' money, he said, "Well, if this deal's *reasonable* I might could...," his voice trailin'; then he pointed out, "I got this damn refrigeration repair to pay for."

Ol' Earl's a terminal tightwad. He makes a damn mint at the club. "Are you shittin' me?" I had to laugh. "Why you got money you ain't even spent yet! And your ol' lady she's a-drivin' a great big Lincoln Continental!"

"Yeah, but I'm still a-drivin' my ol' pickup, ain't I?" he countered.

"And you're still a-fillin' the bed of it up with money to go to the bank, too," said Big Dunc, "chargin' six-bits for a damn puny glass a beer, see."

"You damn rights!" added Hillis.

Earl looked semi-proud, but he shook his head. "I ain't makin' *that* much."

"Listen," Bob Don suggested, "why don't I call this outfit and see what it costs for a raft trip on Kern River."

"Yeah, go ahead," agreed Big Dunc. "You're a-gonna do 'er anyways, see," he said.

Well, he did, that's how come us to be here right next to the river with this young kid named Razz, all of us but cept that chicken Wylie, in bathin' suits — the damnedest collection of pot bellies and skinny white legs you ever seen — while Razz he showed us how to paddle. There was Earl, Dunc, Bob Don, me, my boy Craig, and his pal Junior. Jeffrey he couldn't come on account of he had him a kids' league soccer game. Craig and Junior they never had pot bellies or skinny white legs for some reason, but Dunc he added a little fashion statement because he not only had that world-class beer belly, but he also had forgot to grow much butt, so his trunks they naturally drooped in back just enough to expose that vertical smile.

Anyways, ol' Razz, he was tellin' us this story: "No shit, man, this really happened," he assured us. "Four guys from Bakersfield were coming down the river without lifejackets..." It was a long story, but it seems them boys they hit a rock and got caught in some ropes they had danglin' from their raft and they all drownded deader'n dirt. But that ain't the worst. The cops couldn't get the bodies untangled, so other rafts had to float on by 'em and them bodies they was sorta hangin' there in the water like ghosts, their arms wavin' at the folks floatin' by. It was a *wonderful* story to tell us greenhorns, and all the guys except the two kids looked mighty sick by the time ol' Razz he'd finished.

"Nooooshit?" said Earl in one gasp.

Razz he grinned real big then and asked: "You fellas know the difference between a fairy tale and a river guide's story?" he asked.

We never.

"Well, a fairy tale always starts with `Once upon a time...,' while a guide's story always starts with `No shit, man, this really happened...,' but after that they're the same."

That give us all a chuckle, but our eyes stayed wide.

Razz he was laughin' to beat hell whenever he said, "Come on over here, and I'll get you fellas started. Those slots on the floor are for your feet, to anchor them when we hit rough water." (Bob Don he giggled real nervous whenever he heard that.) "When I say `right,'" the guide went on, "you guys on the right paddle backwards and you guys on the left dig in."

"How the hell can we turn around to paddle backwards if our feet're stuck in them deals, see?" demanded Dunc.

Razz grinned until he realized that Duncan wasn't kiddin'. Just about then he got a inklin' of what he was in for, I reckon. "Just move your *paddle* backwards," he instructed.

"Oh," grunted Dunc. "How come you never said that in the first place, see?"

Razz gazed at him for a second, then went on talkin'. "Anyway, when I say `left,' you guys on the left paddle backwards and you guys on the right dig in." He had us practice that and some other stuff standin' on the shore next to this big raft, and Dunc, he growled out the corner of his mouth, "Shit, this here's kids' stuff. Nothin' to it...easier'n in the army. I wanta hit that damn water, cool off a little bit."

Well, we hit it directly, in this real calm part where ol'Razz he had us practice some more before we got to fast current. "One more thing," the guide added, "if any of you happen to fall in, don't panic — just keep your head and feet up, and point your legs downstream so you can ward off any rocks. Let the current carry you downstream and I'll pick you up as soon as I can."

"Nooooshit?" gulped Earl.

"Unless, of course, you get sucked down into the dark room."

"The *dork* room?" wondered Dunc.

"That's the place where the river's so deep you can't see any light," the guide explained. Then he added, "No shit, man, I was there once."

"The *dork* room!" Dunc said once more.

"It'll be a *dork* room if Duncan gets there," Bob Don chuckled nervously.

"Eat shit," snapped the big guy.

On that encouragin' note we commenced paddlin'. Me, my boy and Junior was on one side, Dunc, Earl and Bob Don on the other. Only trouble was whenever me and the kids set on the raft's sides, our paddles never even touched the water because that beer-bellied crew on the other side outweighed us by a damn ton; we was way up in the air.

"Hey, wait up you guys," laughed Razz. "We've gotta balance this out," and he had Junior switch places with Earl so that the raft it set purty level. "That's better," he smiled.

"Let's get after it, see," demanded Dunc, the raftin' expert.

We moved through this calm section just above some little rapids, and Razz said, "Okay, a little more practice, guys. Left!"

For a second everybody just set there lookin' at each other, then both sides dug in like they was racin' each other and we shot straight ahead toward that fast water while ol' Razz, he hollered, "Wait! Wait!" Too late. It felt like the river it just grabbed the boat and jerked it forward, and my belly swooped like whenever you hit a dip in the road. We hit a rock pretty good and Dunc hollered, "Oooh, shit!" as he tumbled out and his big, yellow life jacket bobbed him to the surface. I also thought I heard a siren but it turned out to be Bob Don, scared and squealin', "Eeeeeeeeeeee!"

Dunc, meantime, looked like a damn walrus, a-sputterin' and a-spoutin'. That water was colder'n a pimp's heart, and Duncan he was a-flailin' to get out. Against our advice, ol' Razz he swung the raft over and pulled the big guy back in soon as we got to slow water. "Wait," I protested, "let us *vote* on whether we let Duncan back in."

"Fuck you," I heard the big guy grunt as he flopped onto the raft's floor. He's graceful too, Big Dunc — his pale white moon there for the world to see until he managed to hoist his 1950s trunks back in place. "You done that on purpose," the shiverin' big guy accused, but Razz ignored him and said, "Now let's try it again before we all drown," and he called, "Left," and we shot forward. He called "Back," and we went in a circle; when he said "Forward," we damn near sunk. Dunc lost his paddle twice — "These damn things're too slick, see," he complained, "not like the ones in the army."

"You're just dick-fingered," I said.

"How'd you like a paddle shoved up your ass," he threatened.

"You don't *have* a paddle, dick fingers," I pointed out — his was floatin' downstream again — "but I do and I just might part your hair with it."

"Fellas, fellas," urged Razz that was beginnin' to look like he wished he'd took some other job, "calm down. We've gotta learn one or two moves here."

"Don't pay any attention to those two," said Bob Don, "they just talk to hear their heads rattle."

"Fuck you!" snapped Dunc and he pushed Bob Don into that freezin' river.

I'll tell you what, ol' Bob Don mighta graduated Bakersfield Junior College, but he never majored in swimmin'. He popped up in his life jacket, spittin' out water and flappin' his skinny arms, but his old Bakersfield Indians baseball cap it was on its way downstream.

"The *Perfesssor* there he looks like a damned drowned rat, see!" called Big Dunc, and he was right.

In fact, Bob Don looked so cold and Dunc was laughin' so hard, that I just reached over with my paddle and give the big guy a teensy nudge. Over he went with a splash like a damn A-bomb, and the raft it damn near capsized. This trip it was turnin' into a hell of a good time.

Meanwhile, Ol' Razz was lookin' semi-frustrated. "Listen, if we don't learn these moves, we won't get to the takeout point by dark. We've been on the river an hour and've only traveled a quarter mile."

Bob Don, out of the water now, sputtered, ""You son of a buck, Duncan! You son of a buck!"

Duncan he was hollerin' at me: "You sumbitch, Jerry Bill. You sumbitch!" His big white belly hung there under the water like a liquid moon, just a-shinin', and this thin string of bubbles it rose up behind him.

"What's that, Duncan," I called, "You spring a leak? We might have to patch ol' Duncan, boys, and pump him up. It appears he's went and sprung a slow leak." Just then a big burst of bubbles surfaced.

"Holy cow," Craig added, "it's a blowout!"

"Screw you!" shivered Dunc.

"Now, now," I said, "there's growin' boys in the raft."

"Screw 'em!"

"These boys don't hear that kinda talk at North High School."

"Screw North High!"

"That Dunc's a real role model," I said.

"Screw role models!"

"With a real big vocabulary," said my boy Craig.

"Screw vocabalaries!"

Craig and Junior that was first-stringers on the football team, they looked at each other and giggled.

"Can't we just get *started?*" appealed Razz. He must of had him a heavy date a-waitin'. I had a feelin' she might have to wait quite a spell.

Eventually we got ourselves down the river, real slow, bumpin' a rock here and there whenever the guide he'd try to get us to paddle left or right, or endin' up facin' the wrong direction. We finally did get that part down and not a second too soon because ol' Razz he said, "There's one more command I want you fellas to remember: 'Hold on!'"

We all laughed.

"I'm not kidding. When I holler `Hold on,' grab those ropes on the sides and flatten your paddle like this, and make sure your feet are in those slots. One other thing, if we find ourselves pushed up against a rock by the current, we've gotta high side — that means just what it says, put all our weight on the high part of the raft and let the water push us free. If you dip toward the low end it'll let in the river and we'll all be swimming," he warned.

111

"Just like we done it in the army, see. I'uz best guy in my outfit at that high-side deal," explained Big Dunc, the assistant guide. "This river ain't shit next to the one I done in the army, see."

"Right," I said and winked at my boy Craig.

Earl, what hadn't said squat, he just rolled his eyes. He looked like he'd just as soon be home in his recliner a-suckin' on a brew and chewin' a toothpick.

The water it was pickin' up speed and we took to bouncin' along that current purty good, Craig and Junior whoopin' and laughin' — "This is great, Razz!" — while we was actually able to go right and left on command most of the time. "Nothin' to this raftin' shit, see," announced Duncan.

Bob Don he never looked too sure. "Don't we have time to pull over and have *one* beer?" he called.

Just then I glanced up ahead and noticed the river disappeared — it just seemed to fall off the edge of the world. All I could see beyond where it dropped was these little white splashes jumpin' up beyond that lip, and I begun hearin' this deep rumble. "What's that?" I asked.

"Ah," grinned Razz, "that's our first big rapid, `The Cauldron.'"

Bob Don's eyes swerved and his voice cracked whenever he said, "The *Cauldron?*"

Earl's lips they turned white.

"Just like when I'uz in the army, see," Big Dunc grinned.

Well, we couldn't see nothin', so it was easy to be brave, but a second later my belly sucked air because the current, it pulled our raft hard like somebody'd switched it into passin' gear, and Razz he hollered, "Right! Right!" Me and Earl and Dunc and Bob Don we just set there like road apples, paddles not movin', our mouths wide open, cause we seen what was ahead — this long white stretch down the canyon where the river it just exploded. I heard Bob Don's siren commence wailin': "Eeeeeeeeeeee!"

"Oooh shit!" me and Dunc and Earl all said at once like the damn Mills Brothers. Bob Don still said, "Eeeeeeeeeeee!"

"Paddle, you guys!" Razz shouted, "*Paddle!*"

Ice-water waves they was splashin' all over us and we was bouncin' this way and that, clean up in the air then — "Boom!" — down in a trough, my butt off the raft then back on it, only my feet in them slots stayin' connected. Soon as we realized it was one of them life-or-death deals, we commenced paddlin' real serious. But by then ol' Razz he was hollerin', "Hold on! Hold on!" Well, the next thing I knew, we was wedged against this big giant rock, half the raft over my head up in the air, the other half fillin' with the whole damn Kern River.

"High side! High side!" called the guide and all except numb-nuts Duncan did. That dumb fart-knocker, he rolled his two-hundred and sixty pounds to the low side and the next thing we was all flounderin' while the raft, the paddles, and Earl's toothpick they all headed on the double downstream toward Bakersfield.

"Eeeeeeeeeeee!"

I wanted to cuss that sumbitch Dunc and to tell Bob Don to shut the hell up, but I had water up my nose and was plenty occupied just a-tryin' to point my feet downstream to ward off them rocks and to find my boy too. I figured we was goners for sure. I couldn't see Craig or Junior nowheres.

Whenever we all finally managed to struggle to shore and tried to round up all our equipment — young Razz actin' real pissed, Craig and Junior lovin' the spill, Bob Don beggin' for a beer, and Earl quiet as a corpse — Big Dunc he went on the offensive. "You guys sure fucked up, see," he asserted. "I had that deal dicked whenever y'all fell out."

Bob Don, shiverin' like a drowned rat but not lookin' nearly that good, he sputtered, "Y-y-you s-s-son of a b-b-buck, D-D-Duncan!"

"Yessir, if you dumb dickheads had just did like me, we wouldn't never a tipped over, see," asserted Big Dunc.

Before the flint-eyed Razz could reply, Craig said, "Big Dunc, hah! Big Dump's more like it!"

Well that broke the tension and even Razz laughed.

"Where's the beer?" asked Bob Don, vibratin' there on his skinny legs that looked like wet pipe cleaners.

"Ask Big Dump," responded Razz. "He dropped it in the river back at the Cauldron. Maybe he'll swim out to find it."

"Yeah Dump, " I added. "Go fetch."

"Screw all you guys," growled the big guy. His face was tan, but his forehead was white as Ivory Soap and these long hairs that he always combed across his dome they all hung way down over one ear like a bunch of dead worms. Quite a piece of work, Dunc. "I might just have to kick somebody's ass d'rectly, see," he added.

Finally, Earl spoke up: "You might just have to float your own fat ass all the way to Oildale in that life jacket if you don't shut your trap. You could fuck up a two-car funeral, Dunc...I mean, Dump."

Junior he looked at Craig and grinned, pointed at Duncan's rear, then said, "Big Dump better hope a cop doesn't come by, because he's showing about fifty pounds of crack."

Them two boys chuckled and punched each other's shoulders and Duncan he growled, "How's that?"

The boys never answered. They just kept lookin' at one another, then gigglin'.

Ever defiant, Big Dunc tugged his droppin' trunks up so only about a foot of his pale ass-slash showed, then glared at us. "Yeah, well none a you guys coulda cut it in my outfit back in the army, see. That'uz a rough deal."

"Yeah, I know," the shiverin' Bob Don Bundy said, "handing out underpants to recruits for two years is a real dangerous assignment."

Craig, that was standin' behind the big guy, he added, "You should've saved a couple of pairs of shorts for yourself, Dump. The ones you're wearing now're causing a crack up." Him and Junior they laughed to beat hell again.

The big guy glared at the boys, then at me, growlin', "You might could teach that kid a yours some manners before somebody kicks his little ass, see."

I grinned. "Yeah, I can't seem to do a thing with him. Maybe a tour a duty in the army'd straighten him out."

"You damn rights," Big Dump nodded, "it done me the world a good, see."

"We can all be grateful for that," I agreed and everyone laughed, but we quit laughin' directly.

"Okay, guys," called Razz, "okay. Time to get back on that water. We're got two more big rapids to go and we'll be at the takeout point: Devil's Roller Coaster and the Guillotine."

"The *Guillotine*," gasped Bob Don.

The two boys said, "Great!"

"The Devil's damn Roller Coaster! The damn Guillotine!" gulped Big Dump. "Well, I'm a-walkin' 'er, see," he announced, and right away commenced hoofin' down the river trail.

There went the army's greatest rafter; I reckon he'd decided to join the infantry. ▤

The Great High School Reunion

I guess Big Dunc had come home shitfaced one time too often, because ol' Dee Dee, his wife, she'd finally went and kicked his ass out. The War Department, as he called her, she'd told him to lay off the beer if he wanted to come home. Naturally, Duncan he was indignant as hell, slurpin' suds at the Tejon Club that afternoon, givin' ol' Dee Dee seven kinds of hell, since she wasn't there. "No damn woman's a-tellin' me what to do, see! I'll just find me another'n is what I'll find. There's lotsa babes out there hot for me, see. Just wait till the damn War Department sees me out with a looker!"

Bob Don Bundy he winked at me, then said, "Well, heck a mile, Duncan, I've got this free-advertiser paper with personals in it. Let's see what we can find for you." He rattled that little paper real good, then said, "Ahhh, here we go, 'GBM, seeks GWM, 25-35, for play.' Then it gives a number."

Duncan he glanced at Bob Don, then grunted, "What's that GBM deal, a German car?"

"Well, it'll give you a ride," grinned Bundy. Me, I laughed.

"Can't you never answer a damn question direct, you little piss-ant? Gimme a straight answer, see," threatened the big guy.

Still grinnin', Bob Don he explained: "It means gay black male seeks gay white male between 25 and 35 years old for some kind of game — probably 'hide the weenie' or maybe 'kiss the snake.'"

Me, I couldn't resist, so I added real sad, "Oh hell, Dunc can't answer thatun on account of he's too old. Tough luck, Duncan."

Earl that runs the joint, he liked to busted a gut laughin', but the big guy he just scowled at me. "You might could get yer ass kicked too, Jerry Bill, see," he threatened.

"You better give me a coffee, Earl," I called. "I'm gettin' all faintified now that Dunc's went and threatened me."

"Now listen here...," Dunc menaced, but Bob Don cut him off.

"You listen, Duncan," he said, "tall, slender, busty elegant SWF who loves to cuddle. Adventuresome spirit, radiant soul, wishes to be loved and spoiled by affluent, kind generous gentleman. Age unimportant."

"No shit?" said Earl. "What's *her* number — it is a '*her*' ain't it?"

Dunc demanded, "What's that SWF deal mean?"

"Single white female, and that one even sounds good to me," added Bob Don.

"Sounds like a hooker to me," I said. "Sounds like she'll cuddle for money is what she'll do."

Earl, that's affluent and a tightwad to boot, he give me a sour look. "You have to go and spoil ever' damn thing, don't you, J.B."

"I don't get it, see," said Dunc who usually don't. "Neither does Earl...not if he has to pay for it," I said. He's the damn world champ at stingy.

Bob Don he chuckled but he kept lookin' down. He was scannin' that paper for more good ones. "Hey, listen to this!" he called. "'Bi-WF seeks same for an understanding and discreet relationship. Loves leather. No males or couples please.'"

"Those're gettin' better," I said.

"I don't get it, see," said Duncan.

"Listen to *this* one, Dunc," called Bundy. "It sounds like it's meant for you. 'It could be that someone you've been looking for. SWF loves c/w & 50s music, dancing, good wine, big men, French and Greek...'"

"That's perfect for Dunc," I said. "He's a geek."

Duncan grinned, "Who's a fuckin' geek, see?"

Earl perked up again. "Do you gotta talk French and Greek for that gal? If you don't, she sounds good to me. What's the number on that one?"

"Besides, what's a fuckin' geek, anyways?" demanded Dunc.

"I don't think the ad was referring to your linguistic skills, Earl," chuckled Bob Don. "Besides, you're married," he said. "We're trying to help that gay bachelor, Duncan."

"Watch the *gay* shit, see," warned the big lunk.

"He meant happy-go-lucky, numb-nuts," I explained.

Just then Wylie Hillis busted in the door. "Gimme a tallun, Earl," he called before he even reached a stool. "The missus's been a-workin' my ass off today and I'm drier'n the damn Sierra Desert."

Bob Don was already grinnin'. "Here's one for Wylie!"

"One what?" the ol' Arkie called.

"Just listen," advised Bundy. "'Mature SWF seeks snuggle bear for romantic evenings, Harley rides, craziness. I am down-to-earth, honest, caring, enthusiastic, outgoing, affectionate, and willing to try new things. Are you?'"

119

Wylie'uz grinnin' whenever he asked, "What's that deal all about?"

"I don't get it, see," said Duncan.

Earl asked, "What's *her* number?" His toothpick was jumpin'.

"You're terminally horny, Earl," I said.

"Mind your own damn business, J.B."

"You ought to run an ad yourself, Earl," suggested Bob Don Bundy. "Why, a businessman like you could probably rope a good-looker."

Earl he looked real thoughtful. "How much you figger somethin' like that'd run?" he asked. "You reckon it's high?"

"He'd do good till a gal got a look at him, anyways, see," grunted Duncan while Earl was talkin'.

"What's that?" snapped the owner.

"Oh, nothin'," grinned Dunc, real pleased with hisself.

"Yeah," fanaticized Bob Don, "I can just read it now, 'ROF, hung like boar mouse, seeks anything that'll screw.'"

"What's that ROF deal?" asked the proprietor.

"Rich old fart," giggled Bundy.

"Listen, knothead," warned Earl, "you're about to become KOA, a knocked-out asshole," and he smacked his toothpick against one palm like it was his attitude adjuster.

Bob Don kept grinnin' but he never said no more.

"Say, Wylie," asked Earl that he kept up on all the local doin's, "what'd the doc have to say yesterday?"

"He said my prostrate was enlarged and he give me some medicine. And he said I had to bring him one of them stool-sample deals and a urine sample too."

"That oughta be easy," I said, "just show him your drawers."

Bundy he winked at me and said, "Your prostrate? I wouldn't take that lying down if I were you..." and he chuckled.

"What's all that?" Wylie he never caught on.

"Said what?" asked Duncan.

"Said my damn prostrate is swole up and that's why I pee about twenty times a night and it don't but trickle," explained Hillis.

"That's because you're tryin' to pee through that zipper in your coveralls," I suggested.

"Hell, I pee all the time too, see," asserted Big Dunc.

I couldn't resist sayin', "Because you got a gut fulla beer."

"Eat shit."

"Hell, I've took to peein' real regular at night myself," Earl said. "Usta be when I was a young buck, me an Momma'd screw about ten times a night and I'd never pee. Now I pee about ten times a night and we don't hardly never seem to screw. Maybe I oughta go see the doc too."

"At least you're active, " I pointed out.

"Sounds like to me that you need to run an ad," opined the college graduate. "You start getting some nooky again and the urinating will take of itself."

"Urinatin'!" exclaimed Dunc, and he laughed. I reckon he figgered ol' Bob Don he'd just made that word up.

Hillis looked real solemn when he said, "Well, that prostrate exam's a real rough deal, boys."

"What's the doctor do?" asked Bob Don real innocent, but I could tell by his expression that he already knew. He just wanted Wylie to tell us.

"Well, she's real rough, I'll tell ya that much."

"But what *exactly* does the doctor do?" insisted Bundy, just the hint of a grin on his face.

"Well, I'll just *show* you what, *Perfesssor*, if you keep a-pushin'," threatened the ol' Arkie.

"What *does* the doc do?" wondered Duncan.

"He sticks his finger up your you-know-what," grinned Bob Don.

Dunc he gasped, "No shit!"

121

"That's what the doc' hopes," said Bob Don.

"That's why ol' Wylie he goes back so reg'lar," I suggested, "gives him a thrill."

"I'll give you a damn thrill, J.B.," snapped Hillis, startin' to sound genuinely pissed. "These golden years ain't all they're cracked up to be, boys, I'll tell ya that much. It's like bein' pecked apart real slow by chickens."

Well, of a sudden, he looked sad, so I changed the subject. I never wanted to hurt his ol' Arkie feelin's. "Hey, did you guys read about the big reunion they're plannin' at the high school?"

None of 'em but cept Bob Don had. The paper it'd said that the Bakersfield High School Foundation was sponsoring this series of decade-reunions to raise money for the school, and the 1950s group was supposed to get together at the gym next month. Me, Dunc, Bob Don, and Earl had all graduated high school there in the '50s.

Well, after we'd discussed it, I said, "Me 'n' Heddy're goin'. How 'bout you, Earl? You could leave the wife home and run an ad, bring whatever it snags. But don't mention your big ol' prostrate."

"Screw you, Jerry Bill."

"Skeeter and I plan to go," Bob Don said.

"We oughta see some of the guys we used to run around with, like ol' Harold and Hinojosa," I said.

"That Hinojosa was one tough little *hombre*," nodded Earl.

"And ol' Harold'uz wild as a peckerless possum," I added. "Them two always made a pair, and they fought each other about as quick as they took on the world. I wonder what they're up to now?"

"In the pen' prob'ly, see," said Dunc. Both of them had kicked Dunc's big ass back in high school, so he wasn't no fan of theirs.

"You goin', Duncan?" I asked.

"I damn sure am," he replied, " and I'm a-gonna pick up on one a them good-lookin' honeys from high school that I shoulda married. There was a hell of a bunch of 'em after me, see. I'll teach that damn War Department!" There he slouched at the bar, a model from that damn *Playgirl* with his belly obscurin' his belt buckle, his ass-crack airin' out in back, a real charmin' deal.

Whenever the big night finally come, me and Heddy we dressed to the teeth, and drove over with Bob Don and Skeeter. Who do you think we seen soon as we got inside? Harold and Hinojosa and their wives that we'd never met before. The whole bunch of us we grabbed a table together, and before long Earl and his top-heavy missus they joined us.

Harold he was on a roll right from the git-go. "That last reunion that you guys never come to," he said, "it wasn't squat. They never give us but these little shitassed glasses for the beer. I liked to passed out from exhaustion just walkin' back and forth for refills."

"That Okie," said Hinojosa, pointing at Harold, "found an empty cottage cheese carton and he made the guy fill it."

"Damn rights," Harold grinned with that swerved mouth of his.

Hinojosa wasn't finished. "Of course, it wasn't everybody got those little glasses," he hissed, like he was whisperin' so the ladies wouldn't hear. "They gave 'em out by dick size, so I got a big mug but this Okie he only got a thimble."

My wife, Heddy, she rolled her eyes, and Harold's wife blushed.

"Your Mescan ass!" snorted Harold.

Before the night's first fight could break out, I stood and said, "Excuse me." Harold and Hinojosa got up too.

"Time to drain the stallion," grinned Harold.

On the way back from the john, Harold he suggested, "Hey let's look around the school before we go back."

Beer was already workin' in us and we was a little loose, wanderin' half-tight in front of the principal's office — a room my companions had visited plenty in the old days. "I always wanted to piss on that door," Harold announced.

"Me, I wanted to piss on the principal," said Hinojosa. "That focker gave me swats, man." There wasn't no lights in the hall but cept these real eerie safety lights. "This place looks like a focking morgue, man," added Hinojosa.

We stopped in front of the trophy case down the hall. "We had us a hell of a team our senior year, boy," Harold bragged.

"Kicked ass, man," his pal agreed.

"Hey," I smiled, "we never won but two games and tied one."

"Bull!" snapped crazy Harold. "We was tough, J.B."

"Naw," I insisted, "it only seems like that 'cause we managed to beat *somebody*. We never beat nobody the year before."

"You sure?" Hinojosa narrowed his eyes at me.

I only grinned. No need to antagonize them.

"Seems like to me we was hell on wheels," Harold insisted.

Hinojosa nodded and said, "The good old days, man. The good old days..."

"No not *that* good," I said. "What made 'em seem so good is that we'uz young and fulla juice."

Harold stopped, put his hands on his hips, and gazed at me a moment. "Listen at him, Hinojosa," he said. "Damn Hogsett's turned into a *philosopher* or some damned thing. Kids today ain't diddly squat. I got boys that don't even play football. One wears a damn *earring*! Spends all his time readin' books! I don't know where we went wrong."

"Mine, too," his old buddy added, "and long hair."

I could only smile at these uncomfortable fathers, who had been the school's rowdies in their youths. Their exploits were probably being discussed that very moment at a lot of tables: the jockstraps they had worn as nose guards to a football awards banquet; the cow turd they had gift-wrapped and presented to the pompous music teacher; the *object d'arte* they had created with inflated rubbers and slipped into the parents' night display in this very building; the sophomore class president they had pantsed and whose ass they had painted because he was a brown-noser.

"Come on, you guys," I said, "we'd better get back to the reunion before our wives leave us."

Harold grunted, "No such luck." His wife had been a hot number, I seem to remember, but now she'd got Born Again, so she never wore no makeup and had on a dress up to her neck and down to her ankles.

"Yeah, I need more beer, man," Hinojosa said.

We sounded like them Spanish flamingo dancers as we clicked the heels of our cowboy boots up the hall back toward the all-purpose room.

Whenever we walked back in, this agin' personality kid (that in high school had walked a mile out of his way to avoid ol' Harold and Hinojosa) he was at the microphone askin' folks to applaud for who looked youngest, who had the least hair, the biggest belly...that stuff. It was downright brutal.

As tough as Harold and Hinojosa were, neither of them looked half as rough as Heddy did whenever we sat down. She'd been stuck makin' polite conversation with Harold's Born-Again wife that was seethin' over his regression into beer, and with Mrs. Hinojosa that never spoke too much English. Mr. and Mrs. Earl, plus Bob Don and Skeeter, they'd drifted away from the table. "Welcome back," my wife said to me, but her voice it sounded like a rattlesnake buzzin'.

125

That master of ceremonies he kept after it, askin' which classmates had traveled farthest to attend the reunion, and which had the most kids. Me, I tuned him out and tried to make up with Heddy. "How're you and Mrs. Hinojosa gettin' along, Babe?"

"My three years of high school Spanish are finally coming in handy," she managed with a smile so ambiguous that I'll bet that's where that Eye-talian, ol' Leonard what's-his-name, got that Mona-Lisa look. Only a wife at her husband's reunion could begin to savvy it.

Time to change the subject, so I asked ol' Earl that'd just come back to the table, "Do you remember whenever these two locos drove over to East High with Rich Etcheverry and took on a carload of guys? That was the big battle of '56."

"Hey, I do," said Bob Don that moseyed up while I was talkin'. "These dang guys had more guts than a slaughterhouse."

Hinojosa raised them V-shaped eyebrows, nodded at his Okie pal, and said, "That focker *loves* to tell it, man."

"Oh, hell, I've forgot that ol' shit," said Harold. Well, he did love to tell it. I could tell that by the way he grinned like a bear eatin' ants. He was still half-hardlookin', Harold, his thin face covered with shiny ridges where he used to have acne. Still lean and muscular too, while Hinojosa was stockier and darker, lookin' like a bodybuilder. His arms were covered by homemade tattoos — he wasn't much of a artist either.

"My wife'd really like to hear about it," I said.

"Yes," she said, her voice like sandpaper scrapin' dirt.

"Well," Harold finally give in, "me and ol' Richard and Hinojosa here..."

"*That* again," spit Mrs. Harold, that seemed a tad short of Christian charity where her ol' man's exploits was concerned.

"*Que paso?*" asked Mrs. Hinojosa.

126

"Te voy a traducir un cuento por este Okie pendejo," replied her husband real pleasant.

"Well, anyways," Harold began once more, "me and Richard and this Mescan we was drivin' around that afternoon and drinkin' Country Club. Richard and his steady gal, ol' Velma Steele, they'd broke up, so he'uz feelin' 'bout half mean. One of us said, 'Let's go over to East High and kick some ass.'"

"You, Pendejo, you said it!" grinned Hinojosa, then he turned to his wife and explained, *"Hace viente or vientecinco anos, con un otro amigo que se llama Richard Etcheverry, Harold y yo fuimos a Bakersfield, y ese gringo loco ha dicho, `Vamos a azotar algunos nalgas.'"*

She giggled and looked at Harold, who winked at her, then he took a pull from his beer.

"It don't matter, 'cause we did end up over there and we seen this car and guess who's drivin' it?"

We couldn't guess, and Hinojosa urged, "Tell 'em, focker."

"It's that Lloyd Dillard, that he was a real good colored fullback for the Blades. Well, since they'd kicked our butts so bad in football, ol' Richard flipped him off and he right away pulls over. D'rectly they took to arguin' and, lemme tell ya, they're both tough as cafeteria steak.

"Now ol' Dillard he has this one other mean-lookin' colored boy in the car with him, so me and this Mescan we feel obliged to choose that guy. Only trouble is, that guy he sets there with this great big ol' arm hanging out the window and this face like a tiger, so I says to Hinojosa, 'He's your meat, buddy. I'm right behind ya.' I kinda back up a step to give him room to work. Trouble is, ol' Hinojosa ain't near as dumb as he looks."

Hinojosa grunted, "Fock you."

"Naw, whenever he seen that great big arm and that mean face, ol' Hinojosa he says to me, 'That's okay, buddy. You can have him.' Hinojosa, he backs up *two* steps."

Hinojosa, by this time, was shakin' his head. "Bullshit!" he said, then looked toward his wife and explained, "*En East Bakersfield, Richard y un negro muy fuerte se fueron a los moquetes. Ese pendejo y yo veiamos un otro negro que tenia un brazo grande y un carra como un tigre. Harold tuvo mucho miedo de el.*"

"Oh," said Mrs. Hinojosa, one hand fluttering to her considerable bosom.

"Are they talking about the same fight or is my Spanish that bad?" my wife she asked me.

Harold was into his story then. "Wellsir," he continued, "that ol' boy's arm looked bigger all the time, so I says to this scared Mescan, 'Naw, you're the one that's gonna join the army and go airborne. You can take him.' I dropped back *three* paces so Hinojosa could move real free.

"'That's okay,' he says to me, soundin' faint, like he might cry, 'you said you was gonna join the marines. He's yours.' That stumped me for a minute, then I told him, 'Well, I would, but I got this bad back,' slippin' back a step or two.'

"'I got a cold,' this Mescan fairy he says, then he fakes a cough and slips behind me. By now, we're 'bout fifty yards from that car and still pullin' away."

Mrs. Hinojosa glanced at her husband, who was shaking his head and mumbling. He translated for her: "*Harold era muy espantando del negro, asi yo dicho, 'Calmese, vato, calmese. Te voy a salvar.'*" His wife beamed at him and patted one of his thick, decorated forearms.

"Are you *sure* they're talking about the same fight?" Heddy wondered aloud.

"Meanwhile, ol' Richard and Dillard they've fought up one block and down another'n and I've damn near run out of excuses. I sure never counted on ol' Hinojosa lettin' me down like that." He paused and took a pull from his beer.

"Just then that great big black guy he got tired of seeing us crawfish, so he opened the car's door and got out all cocky. I figger this Mescan and me're dead men. Then I notice that he ain't *that* much bigger'n us, and that giant arm wasn't so big after all. It's just been flattened against the door.

"'Don't worry, Hinojosa,' I says. 'I won't let that guy hurt ya. I got him,' and I right away take off after that booger.

"'He's mine,' shouts Hinojosa, and he grabs me and pulls me back.

"'Your ass,' I tells him, and I push Hinojosa outta my way, but this dumb Mescan he grabs me and we commence to wrestlin' over who's gonna kick that colored guy's ass. I have to pop him a couple times just to help him get his priorities straight."

Hinojosa's slanted eyes narrowed, and he hissed with an evil grin, "Bullshit! This *pinche* Okie got in my way, so I hit him in the mouth and told him to move off while I kicked that *mayate's* ass." He turned to his wife and said, "*Cuando yo atace ese negro voluminosos, este cabron miedoso estorbo, asi yo te un golpe en la boca.*"

This time Mrs. Hinojosa's hand fluttered to her own *boca*, and her eyes widened.

"*That's* bullshit!" corrected Harold. "This runt just got in my way."

"Fock you, man! I always had to finish things."

"Your ass!" Harold was on his feet.

"You gonna sit down, you Okie focker, or you want me to *knock* you down?" growled Hinojosa, rising slowly, his thick shoulders hunched.

Harold's coat went flying and his wife shrieked like she was at a revival.

"You never was nothin' but a pop-off, *Pendejo*," snarled Hinojosa as he shrugged off his own jacket. They leaned toward one another, face to face, posing like tomcats.

I clasped Heddy's hand and pulled her toward the dance floor — music had just begun — as Hinojosa poked

Harold's chest, and the taller man said, "I stomped your Mescan butt then and I'll stomp it now."

The battlers they surged outside to the parkin' lot with Earl, Bob Don, and a bunch of other grinnin' drunks followin'.

Just then I noticed Big Dunc swagger in the door. He was all dolled up: fancy western shirt, new boots and jeans, plus this great big belt buckle that he couldn't see because of his beer belly. He seen me, give me a little wave, then swerved to the bar for a snort.

While he was standing there surveyin' the scene, who should swish through the door lookin' like a million bucks — hair all bee-hived, high boots, short skirt, boobs bouncin' real sassy? None other than his wife, Dee Dee, the War Department herself. And she wasn't alone. Nope, she was on the arm of Richard Etcheverry — I'd recognize him anywheres.

Dunc's jaw dropped, then I seen him toss down the last of his drink, square his big shoulders, and head for them two.

"I b'lieve there's gonna be a double-header in the parkin' lot," I told my wife.

Heddy just shook her head. "Just like old times," she said. "Happy reunion." ▆

The Great New-Age Deal

Dunc he swaggered into the Tejon Club that afternoon a-wearin' this cap with "God, Guns and Guts Made America Great" printed on the front.

Whenever I seen it, I said, "They give you the wrong hat there Duncan."

"Wrong hat?" he said.

"Yeah, in your case, it oughta be 'God, Guns and *Gut*....'"

That give the boys a laugh, but ol' Dunc he just grunted, "Eat shit."

The next thing you know, though, we was talkin' guns because Duncan claimed he'd bought him this fancy .30-06. He said he was gonna take it up to Greenhorn Mountain come huntin' season and bag him a buck. "I gotta get my deer, see," he said, quite the outdoorsman.

Well, he hadn't bagged nothin' but a six-pack at Wally's Liquor in years. I knew he wasn't no hunter, but he gets on these kicks and purty soon he takes to believin' his own bullshit. Around Oildale, seems like every guy has to at least claim to be a deer hunter, or he ain't a real man.

Anyways, Big Dunc not only couldn't walk up a anthill without needin' oxygen, but he couldn't shoot worth a shit either, so I said, "What's this huntin' bit, Duncan? I been out to the target range with you a time or two, and the safest place to be is in front a the target. You couldn't hit a elephant with birdshot."

"Your ass!" he snorted. "Back in the army I'uz a damn sharpshooter, see. The best in my damn outfit."

Bob Don that was slightly of the liberal persuasion like all your college types, he liked to rag us whenever it come to the right to bear arms. "What do you guys need with guns anyway? Insecure? Penis envy?"

"Huh?" said Dunc, a typical comeback. "What's that penis deal, anyways?"

"We need 'em because our forefathers told us to, Bundy," I snapped. "It's in the Constitution, by the way!" I wasn't takin' no lip off of him.

"You need a musket, then, that's what our forefathers were talking about, not machine guns or automatic pistols or semi-automatic rifles. Those didn't even exist when they wrote the Bill of Rights. And you'd better join the National Guard, too, since the Second Amendment refers to a militia not an individual."

"Oh yeah," snapped Duncan. He was really on his toes.

"Why don't you guys knock it off," urged Earl that'd heard us on this subject before.

"They never wrote nothin' about any muskets, they said *firearms*," I pointed out.

"They said the right to bear arms, *period*," Bundy countered, "if you want to be technical, and arms in those days meant muzzleloaders."

"Oh, balls!" I said. Your liberals won't talk reasonable.

"Well, I'm a-gonna get me my buck, see," groused Duncan into his beer. "And I'll carry all the damn guns I want..."

Earl that runs the joint, he slid out the pump .12-gauge shotgun he kept under the bar, then the .357 magnum he had in a slot by the cash drawer, and he said, "You guys shut the fuck up." He never did nothin' but show 'em to us, but he made his point. He was a-tryin' to watch news on TV.

We shut up and Earl put his hardware away.

On the screen, some gal she was interviewin' this other gal that she was a ranger at this place where there was this big colony a barkin' seals — noisy as hell. Anyways, that ranger gal she grinned into the camera and said, "The bull elephant seals spend most of their waking hours trying to mate with the cows."

Big Dunc that was slurpin' a brew at the bar, he piped right up, "Just like me, see, them bulls, spend the whole damn day a-matin'."

Earl he couldn't resist: "Yeah, I seen some of the elephant seal cows you dated back in high school, Duncan. You and them seal bulls got more than double chins in common."

"Oh yeah," snapped Dunc — his usual clever reply. Instead of arguin', he tried to divert attention away from his own pitiful teenage love life: "Oh yeah! Well you shoulda seen the dogs ol' J.B. there usta take out, see."

He couldn't resist gettin' me into it, I guess, but I just ignored him. He's like talkin' to one a them elephant seals —all bark — so there ain't no point.

"Hey, Jerry Bill, guess who's back in town?" asked Bob Don Bundy, all pals again, and with this silly look on his face like a dog that found a fresh cat box.

I just shrugged. "Beats hell outta me," I answered. I mean, how do you answer a question like that?

"Earl?" asked Bob Don, tryin' to get somebody to give him a guess.

"How the hell do I know?" grunted Earl.

"Dunc?"

"Eat shit," grunted Big Dunc.

"Who?" I finally asked.

"Nedra Marie Dubarry Wilhite is who!"

"No lie!" I couldn't hardly believe it.

"Does Shoat know?" asked Earl. He was referrin' to ol' Nedra Marie's ex-husband that'd had her run outta town a few years back whenever he caught her and this young boyfriend dippin' into the till, among other things.

"She better hope not," I said. That's a fact because ol' Shoat's tough as a Mexican family — and that's *damn* tough.

Bob Don he was still grinnin'. "And guess what else I heard?"

Dunc cut the cheese.

"Is that your guess?" asked Bundy.

"That's the smartest thing you'll hear from him," I said.

"Eat shit, see," grunted Duncan.

"I heard she claims she's a *medium* now," said Bob Don with a grin.

"I'd'a said she'uz a large," grunted Big Dunc. "Specially her tits, see."

"Duncan," said Bob Don Bundy, "you've got a mind like a race horse: It runs best on a dirt track."

"Eat shit," come back that silver-tongued Dunc.

Earl he scratched his head and munched a handful a beer nuts. "What the hell kinda *medium* you talkin' about?"

"Well, I saw this ad in a little throwaway paper that had her picture in it and it said she was a 'New-Age Healer and Psychic' visiting from Texas."

"No shit?" I said. Me, I'd read in the newspaper about that New-Age deal.

"Yeah," he went on, "it said she's going to give a free lecture at the Veterans' Memorial Hall tonight and she's going to talk about fire walking. A tickler, I'd guess, to draw people in. You guys want to go?"

"That ain't her favorite kinda tickler, see," snorted Dunc, that can come up with a goodun ever' once in awhile. I had to laugh.

That encouraged Duncan, so he snapped that paper outta ol' Bob Don's hands, stared at it and chewed on the words a minute, then asked, "What the hell's a `physic'?"

"It's what you need," answered Bob Don, grabbin' back his newspaper. "Any of you guys want to go hear Nedra Marie talk about fire walking?" he asked.

The Tejon Club it ain't but a short mile from the Vet's Hall, so I said, "Why not?"

"I don't get it what it is she's supposed to do," said Earl.

Since I'd read about that New-Age scheme in the paper, I knew the answer to that one. "It's this latest deal to make money that they come up with, kinda like the old tent preachers but for rich folks."

"I still don't get it," admitted Earl, toothpick alert.

"It's just that people are willing to pay for almost anything," Bob Don explained, "even the illusion that they're getting better or younger or stronger or some such when they know they aren't. In fact, that's when they pay the most."

"Those Yuppie deals got more money than good sense," I said.

"What I mean is what do they *do?*" insisted the proprietor.

"Play with each other, see," Dunc grumped. I knew he didn't have a clue, but he wasn't too far off that time.

"All kinda silly stuff," I said. "Pretend they're someone else, do this Chinese shit, beat drums, play like they're babies..."

"Play doctor," interjected Dunc — one-track mind — but I ignored him and kept explainin' to Earl.

"...mess with crystals, walk on fire, even take these high colonic deals."

"What's that, them `high-colonic deals'?" asked Wylie Hillis that he'd just walked in. "It sounds rank to me," he added.

"That's an enema," said Bob Don.

"A *enema!* No shit?"

"Lotsa shit," grinned Dunc. He's on a damn roll, just fulla cute remarks.

"It sounds crazy as hell to me," Earl grunted.

Just then the telephone rang and Earl he shuffled over and answered it. He got this grin on his face, then said, "Hey Dunc, it's the War Department." Him and Dee Dee was back together.

Big tough Duncan flinched like someone'd slugged him, and he whispered, "Tell her I just left, see."

"He just left," Earl said into the phone.

Still grinnin', Earl held that phone away from his ear for what seemed like a long time and we could all hear this midget voice buzzin', then he hung up. "She says the insurance man's at the place and you was s'posed to be home to talk to him and get your big ass home."

"Oh yeah!" said Dunc, real defiant. But he was slidin' off his stool and suckin' down the last dregs of his draft. A second later he scooted out the door.

"By damn," Wylie Hillis grinned around his unlit pipe, "ol' Dunc's sure got that woman under control," and we all had a laugh.

"Gettin' back to that Nedra Marie Dubarry Wilhite deal, we oughta at least go see what's up," I suggested.

Toothpick low, Earl asked, "How much you figure that might run me?"

"Free, I think."

"Free? Then let's do 'er," grinned Earl, toothpick high.

That evenin' whenever me and Earl and Bob Don we seen her on stage, ol' Nedra looked younger than a few years back. I believe she'd had ever'thing lifted that'd go up. "Gol dang," said Earl, "that ol' hide's lookin' prime!"

Well, there was this funny music playin' and the hall it was dim whenever Ol' Nedra Marie she walked out in a semi-see-through gauze gown into these blue and red lights. The first thing she done was announce that her "eternal name," as she called it, was "the Very Right Reverend Doctor Ramadama" and that she was this "Ascended Master" deal and that she'd had these six past lives: She'd been a princess and a king and a wizard and a priestess and a queen and a Aztec virgin. "I figgered it'uz about that far back since she'uz a virgin," I said.

Bob Don sneered, "I wonder if she was Homecoming Queen too?"

Ol' Earl, he whispered, "She never mentioned that she'd been a crook and stole that money from Shoat Wilhite."

"Nobody ever seems to remember being a hooker or a gravedigger or a day laborer," hissed Bob Don. "They were all kings and queens and high powers."

"Me too," I grinned.

"You're still a queen," Earl grinned real evil when he said that, and even I had to laugh.

Anyways, ol' Very Right Reverend Doctor Ramadama she give a long talk all about this "empowerment" deal and how this new age deal it was comin' and everyone was gettin' stronger and spirits they was fixin' to talk to us. She got me to laughin' whenever she flashed this slide on the screen of her standin' out in the country and there was this streak on the picture like her camera leaked light. "That," she pointed out, "is a wood nymph that led me to the trees. She's the fairy that dwells in my clan's power spot there and gives me strength to share my enlightenment with you."

Earl he was laughin' too, toothpick bobbin'. "That streak it looks like the time we turned the lights out at the club and lit one of Dunc's farts," he pointed out.

It really did and Ol' Bob Don he said, "That's Dunc's power spot."

"Besides, we brung our own fairy with us," I said to Earl and we both poked Bob Don.

"Screw you guys," he grinned. This was better'n a damn vaudeville show. We got a lotta dirty looks for laughin', but it seemed like nobody wanted to tangle with us 'cause nobody said nothin'.

Pretty soon the Very Right Reverend, she advised, "You must activate your kundalini," she told folks.

"Do what?" asked Earl.

"Activate your wienie," said Bob Don.

Earl he grinned. "Hell, I could go that."

"That's exactly what ol' Earl's wife wants him to do," I added.

What ol' Ramadama — I like that name — never said was that she was workin' on gettin' rich. Her folks was peddlin' all kinds of shit in the lobby: crystal rocks and these funny cards with pictures on 'em and calendars and tapes and books — you name it.

Best of all, though, she said that the very next afternoon this young guy that never had but one name, OmAr (no shit, he really spelled it that way with two capitals — I seen it on a sign in the lobby), he was fixin' to walk on fire and show other folks how to do it, and that they'd get real brave and real successful if they just done like he done. But, of course, it was gonna cost some hard cash.

I seen right away this was like them ol' deals at the carnival that they let you in the tent to see the good-lookin' dancin' gals for a quarter, but if you wanted to see 'em buck naked, you had to shell out another four bits and go behind the curtain. When you did, it was their mother or grandmother that stood there, naked and ugly and bored.

Anyways, the audience it was full of young, kind of rich-lookin' folks, and it seemed like they all had stars in their eyes and drool on their chins. It was like goin' to the Assembly of God for a revival, seein' them glazed eyes, hearin' them shouts of "Yes! Yes!"

Whenever ol' Ramadama introduced OmAr, this expensive lookin' young guy next to me, he said to the gal next to him, "OmAr was a Druid priest who advised King Arthur in a previous life!" That gal she blinked her eyes, all thrilled, and she said, "I heard he was born at Stonehenge."

"No," interrupted this other gal that she overheard 'em, "I heard he just appeared on the summit of Mount Shasta and Ramadama transported him down with psychic energy."

"Oooh," cooed the first gal.

"Oh bullshit," said Earl. Then he added, "I recollect that he usta be a tentmaker back when I'uz in high School — usta activate my wienie most mornin's." Me and Bob Don broke up. One of the PE teachers at Bakersfield High way back when had called them mornin' hard-ons us kids used to wake up with "Omar the Tentmaker." I'd damn near forgot about that.

"If he *is* Omar the Tentmaker, then I got to know him real good back in them days too," I chuckled.

"Who didn't?" agreed Bob Don. "This really is a goofy bunch of people, isn't it. It looks like these son of a bucks'll believe anything Nedra Marie tells them."

Well, dopey or gullible or whatever they was, them folks had filled the parkin' lot with all these big expensive German and Japan cars. It looked like to me they had more money than good sense, and wasn't no one in cowboy boots but us three from the club. I guess we looked strange to them, what with the way some of 'em stared at us then real quick switched their eyes if we caught 'em. We musta been hard-lookin' to them.

Anyways that next day I was in the club after work talkin' to Wylie Hillis. I told him about that fire-walkin' deal and how it was supposed to give folks power.

"Far walkin'," he spit, then shook his head, lookin' real stylish in his faded, zip-up coveralls. "Some folks don't have brains enough to pour piss outta a boot." He looked real disgusted for a minute, then he said, "I'll tell ya, J.B., I recollect one time at a tent meetin' back in Fayetteville I seen these ol' boys that they was dancin' with *snakes* in their mouths. They said God give 'em *par*. In fact, they thought they'uz real parful, but this one ol' boy he got bit and died deader'n a turd. I b'lieve he was a tad less parful than the snake. Is that what that far-walkin' deal does?"

"We'll see, but I think maybe you hit it on the head, though. This's just a way those Yuppie deals can act like Pentecostals without feelin' guilty."

"Ya reckon?" grinned Wylie.

That next evenin', there was another crowd at the auditorium for the fire walkin' and I couldn't resist. It was a goofy mix of folks wanderin' from the parkin' lot — heavy gals in muu-muus and skinny guys in them designer jeans, thin gals in these pantsuits and fat guys in what looked like robes. Before I ever even got inside, though, I seen this one ol' boy maybe my age — no spring chicken — and he was dressed like one of them San Francisco hippies. Wellsir, he was standin' right in front of the door in one of them funny colored T-shirts and a bandana on his long hair; his eyes they looked like pinwheels and he was a-preachin' to whoever's dumb enough to listen, and I was. But just for a minute.

"Free the Oakland Five! We have to like legalize our sacramental LSD," he said. "LSD is like derived from living plants, and it is like our brothers in the vegetable kingdom talking to us humans. It *must* be legalized! It like *must* be! All power to the people! Free the Oakland Five!"

He looked crazier'n a three-peckered goat to me, what with his little pointy beard and all. "Hey pal," I said to him.

"What, man?"

"Free the Indianapolis Five Hundred!" I said, then I winked, made one a them V-for-victory deals with my fingers, and walked away.

"Right on, Brother!" he called after me.

Anyways, at the box office, I found out you could watch the fire walkin' for twenty bucks, but it cost another century note if'n you wanted to trot the coals. I said no thanks on that hundred-bucks part, and went in.

I damned near give up and went home before they finally got to the hot stuff because for a good two hours the Very Reverend Doctor Boobs and ol' OmAr they just talked and preached and cajoled a few more bills from the faithful, but finally ever'one paraded outside to the lawn behind the hall where there was this shallow pit, maybe ten or twelve foot long, and it was filled with what looked like charcoal briquettes. They looked damn hot to me. At the far end, somebody'd filled a kid's plastic wadin' pool with water.

First let me tell you about ol' OmAr: He had one a them A-rab towel deals wrapped around his head, and he was wearin' this gown that it looked like my wife Heddy's housecoat. When he assembled apprentice fire walkers at one end of the pit and was givin' 'em a pep talk, he swished his arms all around in that housecoat like a damn butterfly. I reckoned he might take off any second.

Me, I was with the spectators lined up along the side to watch folks hike them coals. And guess who I of a sudden noticed in the big crowd with me: Shoat Wilhite. He seen me too, so we made our ways to each other, shook hands and exchanged howdies. He's a good ol' boy, Shoat, and I was really glad to see him. He had this other young guy in a suit and tie with him and he introduced him as Jim Fishman, his attorney.

"Jim and I intend to have a word or two with my ex-wife," he told me, and his eyes they went all hard and cold. "I warned her way back when never to come back

here, but I guess she thought I was kiddin'. I wasn't."
Me, I was glad I wasn't the one he was pissed at. He can
be one hard *hombre*, Shoat.

Just then all them apprentices they commenced
chantin': "Cool, wet grass! Cool, wet grass!" and who
should appear but the Very Right Reverend Ramadama
herownself. She exchanged a few inspirational words with
the suckers, then turned and announced to all of us, "I
shall defy the great flames!"

There wasn't no flames but, like I said, them coals
looked hot enough.

Ramadama she swirled around and begun callin',
"Cool, wet grass! Cool, wet grass!" and she d'rectly
stepped right onto the coals just as she noticed Shoat a-
glarin' at her. She forgot the cool grass and hesitated on
them hot coals, almost stumbled, then she said, "Ouuu!
Owww! Eeee!" and hopped into that wadin' pool as quick

as she could, her face suddenly lookin' old, like the one on that naked lady at the carnival all them years ago. Shoat and Jim they buttonholed her right now and marched her — she was limpin' some — back toward the hall.

A lot of the spectators they was laughin', and them apprentices they never looked quite so confident of a sudden. In fact, maybe half of 'em commenced marchin' away despite ol' OmAr's protests: "Find your center! Don't surrender to fear. Empower yourself! Find your cool center!"

Apparently a bunch of 'em thought they'd find their centers somewheres else because they departed.

OmAr he done the best he could to talk the others into crossin' them coals, walkin' across a couple a times real fast hisownself, but only a few turned their faces to stone and hurried across sayin' "Cool, wet grass," then jumpin' into that wadin' pool. The others just drifted away into darkness. The edge had went from the evenin' and the big show it petered out directly. Ol' OmAr he looked like he could use a tentmaker of his own.

Shoat come in the club that next long, hot afternoon and announced, "My ex-wife's gone and her fancy man's packin' up this afternoon. She won't be back...unless she wants to see the inside of the jailhouse."

"Have a brew, Pard'," I said, and he accepted.

Not fifteen minutes later here come my boy Craig and his pals Junior and Jeffrey, and they was laughin' to beat hell. "Hey, Dad," Craig called. "Me and Junior and Jeffrey went over to the auditorium after school to watch them close up that fire walkin' pit and pack up." (I'd told him what I'd seen the night before and he was disappointed he never got to see the fire walkin'.) "Anyway, that Arab guy took his shoes off for some reason, so we took them and put them on the hood of a car in the middle of that big parking lot.

143

We wanted to see if he could walk barefoot across the hot blacktop like all us kids do." He grinned.

"He couldn't," grinned Jeffrey.

Junior added, "You shoulda seen him hop!"

Them three commenced bouncin' on one foot then the other, callin' "Ouch! Eeee! Oooh!" gigglin' and pokin' each other. Then ol' Craig he said, "Maybe he forgot to say `Cool, wet grass.' You know what? Me and Junior and Jeffrey ought to start a pavement-walking class, sorta empower people to walk barefooted in Oildale during the summer the way we do."

"You got it, son," I grinned, real proud. That boy was gonna be rich some day.

"Hey," said Bob Don real serious. "You guys shouldn't make fun of psychics like that. Look what they taught me," and he real quick showed us a crystal and popped it into his mouth and begun crunchin' it. Hell, I thought he'd went nuts — he was gonna break his damn teeth — then he grinned and showed us a plastic bag labeled Rock Candy. "Care for some?" he asked the boys.

While we was helpin' ourselves, Earl he got this real serious look on his puss and he turned to Craig and Junior. "Listen, you young bucks," he told 'em, toothpick real stern, "you better hope you never pissed off that A-rab. If there's anyone kids your age don't wanta piss off it's Omar the Tentmaker. Without him, your whole day might be ruined. Am I right fellers?" he asked us old poops.

"Oh yeah," we agreed.

Then I added, "All but cept Duncan. He might have had guns, God and guts, but he only has him a little pup tent and the pup is usually asleep."

While everyone else was laughin', that silver-tongued Big Dunc grunted, "Eat shit." ▰

The Great X-mas
Controversy

'Twas the week before Christmas and all through the club,
us boys we was watchin'...well, a lousy football game is
what we was watchin'. That's as much of that poetry deal
as I can do, anyways. We had one of them minor bowl
games on the tube, the Draino Toilet Bowl, the Copenhagen
Snuff Bowl, or some such, two teams from the South with 6-
5 records makin' we're-number-one signs into the camera.

The phone rang, and Earl that runs the joint he
answered it, then called, "It's for you, Bob Don. Skeeter,"
he added.

Bob Don he crawled off his stool and took the hand-
set. "Okay, Honey," he said. "All right, Honey. And a
quart of milk? Okay, Darling. Soon. I won't be long. All
right, Baby."

On the windows facing the street, a single, sorry
string of Christmas lights blinked now and then, and a
wilted-lookin' cardboard Santa was taped there too. I said

to that tightwad proprietor, "You never spared no expense on decorations this year, did you, Earl?"

"You ever *buy* any a them lights?" he demanded. "They're *real* high."

"Them things work about as good as ol' Wylie's gear, see," added Dunc. Wylie, he'd made the mistake of tellin' us he'd been to the doc' to see about more plumbin' problems.

"The hell!" snapped that ol' Arkie. "I'll outscrew you, numb-nuts."

We all laughed.

Bob Don he finally hung up, and ol' Dunc that was on the prod for some reason he nodded at him then sneered to me, "Pussy whipped, see. Bundy sure lets his ol' lady boss him around."

"By God," asserted Hillis, glad for the chance to change the subject. "The missus she don't never call me whenever I'm here at the club. She knows better."

Bob Don he set back on his stool and asked, "What's the score now?"

Southern Mississippi had just scored a touchdown and tied Vanderbilt.

"Who's the hell's a-playin'?" Dunc demanded. He'd been watchin' the whole damn game.

Earl he rolled his toothpick, then told Duncan the score.

"Well, them guys ain't worth a rat's ass, see," said the big guy. "Back when I'uz playin' army football, that'uz a rough deal. Me, I'uz the best in my damn outfit."

I looked at Earl, Earl he looked at Bob Don, Bob Don looked at Wylie. I'd played football with Dunc at high school, so I said, "You're still pickin' splinters outta your ass from Bakersfield High. You never got nothin' but pine time because you couldn't play worth a shit."

He couldn't either. Slower'n a damn slug and none too brave, as I recall.

146

"Oh yeah!" the big guy puffed up. "Well, the coach never liked me, see. He liked them coloreds. But in the army, by God, I'uz..."

"We know, you'uz a piss-cutter." I shook my head and grinned.

Just then the telephone it rang again, and Earl he answered it. "Dunc," he said, "your little bride."

"The War Department?" The football star cringed for a second, then said, "I just left."

"He just left."

Earl he stood there for a long time, noddin' and grinnin' and suckin' on that toothpick. Then he hung up. "She says you was supposed to bring laundry detergent home a hour ago and you'd better snap to it d'rectly or she's gonna come over here and get you."

"Oh yeah?" snarled Dunc, defiant as hell now that the War Department had hung up. Then he slipped off his stool and hurried to his pickup.

"That's ol' Dunc," I said. "Back in the army, he'uz the best in his outfit at dealin' with women."

That give ever'one a laugh.

A minute later, the door opened slow, and there stood this ragged, skinny Oriental guy and a couple little kids. I don't remember ever seein' a Oriental in the club before. He held a hat in both hands. "You boss?" he asked, his English soundin' real strange to me.

"Who me? Hell no," Wylie replied. "That guy there is," noddin' at Earl.

"You boss?"

"Yeah." Earl's eyes narrowed. I think he could smell something that might cost him a buck or two. His toothpick went still.

"You got wo'k?" The voice was soft, but the man looked directly at Earl.

"Got what?"

"Wo'k."

147

Earl made a face.

"He means work," Bob Don said.

"Hell no, I cain't pay nobody to do no work."

Bob Don made a face himself...at Earl...then he turned toward that man. "What kind of work do you do?"

"Any. No pay. Food."

"He doesn't want your money, Earl. He just wants somethin' to eat."

"Well, I..."

I reached into my pocket and withdrew a bill; those folks needed food more than I needed another beer. "Give him and his kids each one a them cellophane sandwiches and some chips and a soda pop. On me."

"Well...okay," Earl nodded.

I added, "And give that man a broom to sweep this place so he can feel like he earned it."

"Okay."

He did that and the skinny man carefully swept the Tejon Club. I never seen that floor so clean. His kids stayed with him, not touchin' the food until their daddy he was finished. "You got mo' wo'k?"

"No, I ain't got no more work."

"Wait a minute," I said. "Me and Heddy can scare up a job or two around the place for this guy. How 'bout you, Bob Don?"

"Sure."

"Wylie?"

"I ain't got nothin' for no Chinaman to do."

I turned toward the man and said, "You come on back tomorrow and we'll have some work for you, okay?"

"Oh," he grinned, "nice. Nice. I come." Then he scooped up them sandwiches and sodas and chips and took off.

"Where'd that Chinaman come from?" asked Wylie.

"I don't know," I said, "but I'm gonna find out." I walked to the door.

148

"Hey, you're gonna miss the rest a the game," Earl pointed out.

"Big loss. This time Dunc's right. Even *he* could probably play with them two sorry teams. See you guys later."

That man and his kids had just rounded the corner on Chester Avenue, so I strolled along behind as they hurried along south all the way to the Kern River — or its dry bed, anyways. We'd been havin' a damn freeze and it was colder'n a witch's tit outside. My breath was busting white steam. Them three they climbed the levee and disappeared into what was left of the forest that usta line the stream. I followed 'em but kinda lost track, and then I come around a bend and I seen that man with three women and maybe eight or nine little kids, and they was splittin' them three sandwiches and all, lookin' happy but real ragged and cold.

They also looked real familiar. Whenever my folks come out here from Oklahoma, and I wasn't but a little bitty kid, we'd camped right in these same woods. We'd built us a shelter outta whatever we could find, just like these folks done, and me and my brothers and sisters we was hungry a lot, just like these kids. I have to tell you, it grabbed me damn deep to see folks livin' like that in California in the 1990s. And me with a well-fed family, two cars, two TVs, a nice house, a good job. It got me to thinkin'.

Just then two more men, both of 'em lookin' tired and hungry and sad, they showed up, and some of them kids run up to 'em and laughed. The other guy, he'd saved 'em some chow and give it to 'em and that pepped 'em up some. So it was a whole gang stranded here just like we was whenever we come out lookin' for work way back when.

Whenever I got back to the Tejon Club, Wylie and Earl was into it: "That's X-in' out Christ is what!" insisted Wylie. The ol' Arkie he was pointin' a finger at Earl's face.

149

"Hell, Wylie, I *got* that deal free at the Church of the Nazarene! Or Mildred did. She brung it home from church." The proprietor had went and taped a fancy "Merry Xmas" sign on the mirror over the bar. I kinda liked it.

"Well, by God, the missus she goes to the Assembly a God and the preacher there he told her that that 'Xmas' deal it was X-in' out Christ! He give her a deal to read up on it." Hillis thrust his unlit pipe forward. "And besides, that Santy deal you got in the window, that's really *Satan*! Just look how it's spelt. That's how come him to wear a red suit. That was in the deal the preacher give the missus too."

"Well, that preacher's fulla shit, see," suggested Duncan that was back on his favorite stool. "If you spell that different, it's still s-h-i-t!"

"You're fulla shit, Duncan!" snapped Wylie, his pipe quiverin'...

Yeah, the Christmas spirit — or maybe the *Xmas* spirit — was in full bloom at the club. "Listen, you peckerheads," I said, "I wanta tell you what I just seen." I did that and, to my surprise, nobody laughed, nobody said nothin' mean.

"You mean that little Chinaman and some others're a-livin' out by the river. Hell, I thought that there kinda stuff'uz ancient history," Wylie said.

"They're probably Hmongs," suggested Bob Don. "I read where a bunch of them came here from Fresno hoping to find field work, but the freeze this year killed crops, and there's no work around right now. They're probably stranded."

"What's Hmongs?" asked Earl.

"They're from Vietnam...or Cambodia...or Laos..."

"No shit?" Dunc he seemed interested. "I never seen no Viet Nams that they kicked our butts in that war. I figgered them Viet Nams for great, big bastards, see."

"Little guys," I said, "with wives and buncha little kids — three families it looked like, tryin' to make do right where that ol' Hooverville camp usta be."

"Little guys and they kicked our butts?" Dunc he seemed amazed. "It's a good thing for them *I* wasn't still in the army then, see."

"Right," grinned Earl.

"We gotta help them folks out," I announced and I wasn't jokin'.

Wylie he was lookin' real dubious and he said, "I don't know 'bout no *Viet Nams*..."

"You know about *folks*, don't you? You know about bein' cold and hungry, don't you? You know about little kids without no decent clothes, don't you? That's all you need to know," I snapped, probably stronger than I should've, but his silly "Viet Nams" shit got to me.

"Jerry Bill's right, boys," agreed Bob Don. "Let's figure out what we can do for those families."

"But if they was the ones that went and kicked our butts, see, why should we help 'em?" asked Dunc.

"The ones that're here fought on *our* side, Duncan," explained Bob Don Bundy real slow. He read all the time, and he knew his history real good. "The commies kicked them out for helping us."

"Some of 'em was on our side?" marveled Dunc, the foreign affairs expert. "Well, that's diff'rent, see. What do you wanta do, J.B.?" he asked me.

"I still don't like that X-in' out Christ deal," added Wylie, lookin' for a argument.

I give him a glance that'd kill grass. "Forget that crap!" I barked. Seein' them poor folks out there had me on the prod. I got us back to the subject: "I vote for us givin' them folks a early Christmas," I suggested, "and today we need to scare up some grub for all of 'em."

"How much you reckon somethin' like that might run?" moaned the ol' pennypincher, toothpick droopin'.

151

"How many more a them cellophane sandwiches you got there, Earl?" Hardly nobody ever bought one.

"Well, those're real expensive," he said.

"Bullshit," I said. "Tally up a dozen of 'em, a dozen cokes, a dozen bags a chips — at *your* cost — and us guys'll split it four ways."

"We will?" croaked Wylie.

"You damn rights," agreed Dunc.

Bob Don said, "Certainly."

"I...I guess we will," Wylie finally nodded. Then he mumbled somethin' about "Viet Nams."

Earl he slunk to the sandwich display and begun baggin' food. That toothpick of his it hung at a tragic angle.

Just then the telephone rang, so I answered it, "Tejon Club," I said.

"Is that you, J.B.?" asked Heddy, my wife.

"It sure is, Babe."

"What time will you be home?"

"Before long. Listen, lemme tell you what I seen today." I explained the whole deal to her.

When I finished, she said, "Oh, Jerry Bill, we can't let them live out there like that."

She's a good gal, so I knew she'd say that. Well, she took over callin' the wives while me and Dunc delivered food out to that camp. It was a sad, sad deal, I'll tell you that much, and them folks was sure happy for them crummy sandwiches. One sorry tent was all they had for the whole gang. It seems like they did have two old cars, but one was broke down and they never had money for gas anyways. The little guy that'd come into the club earlier, he said they'd come here hopin' to find work, and that they had kinfolk in Fresno and wanted to get back there.

Well, ol' Dunc he upped and volunteered to have his oldest boy Doyle, that he was a fix-it man, work on that car. I told the Vietnamese guy to bring everyone to the club that next day and we'd have work for 'em all, and that little guy he liked to've bawled he was so happy. "Oh, thank!" he said. "Oh, thank!" and he pumped my hand and Dunc's.

That next day the club it looked like one of them Hollywood-movie Christmases. Heddy and Dunc's bouncy wife, Dee Dee, they'd fixed up a tree; Heddy told me ol' Earl's first words when he seen it was, "How much'd *that* run?"

The gals they set up other decorations, too. And they'd helped Earl's frau, Mildred, and Wylie's missus, Olive, cook up a turkey and all the fixin's. Skeeter, that was Mrs. Bob Don Bundy, her and my boy Craig and his pals Junior and Jeffrey, they went out and bought ever' one of them little kids three presents: a toy, some gloves, and a jacket. Me and the boys bought each one of them adults a jacket and gloves and rounded up a big tent from ol' Bo Simmons. Hey, we all got jobs and it's only money.

And you shoulda seen them little Vietnamese kids' faces whenever they come in the front door. Even ol' miser Earl had to grin. It was worth every damn penny, boys. Every damn penny. Pretty soon Craig and Junior that they was on North High's football team and wearin' their letter jackets, and Jeffrey too, they was tossin' a football — one of the gifts — with the bigger kids. Most of them Vietnamese kids was wearin' their new jackets and gloves right there in the club.

Directly we all ate turkey and pumkin pie. Then a surprise come: Ol' Cletus Rollins, preacher at the Assembly of God, and B.J. Mayfield, preacher at the Church of the Nazarene, they showed up — the first time they'd ever been in the Tejon Club — and they brung three big boxes of clothes, and some groceries too. That was real good of 'em. I have to admit, I've thought different of them churches ever since. Directly, Heddy and Skeeter took to teachin' the little kids to sing Christmas carols and them kids they caught right on.

Pretty soon I seen Dunc and his dainty little wife, that hadn't been reconciled all that long, lookin' all starry-eyed together, Skeeter and Bob Don they was all cooned-up, and even Wylie and the missus looked like they was about to snuggle. But I was wrong about ol' Wylie.

For whatever reason, he decided to buttonhole Earl again and, like a broke record, start in on him: "I still think you oughta take down that X-in' out Christ deal, Earl," asserted the Arkie, pointin' at the offendin' "Merry Xmas" proclamation. "It's a damn sin is what it is."

Before Earl could say anything, Heddy detached herself from my arm, smiled, and patted Wylie's shoulder. "Don't worry about Christ, Wylie," she smiled. "He's here." And she nodded toward them happy folks with their food and their presents.

Then Heddy M. Hogsett, my wife, she walked right back to me and kissed me in front of God and everyone. "I'm proud of you, J.B.," she said.

"Me, too, Dad," said Craig, and that big lunk that he was first string on the high-school football team, you know what he done? He hugged me right there.

Well, I felt funny, like my throat had went soft and my eyes was warm. But to tell you the truth, I was semi-proud of myownself. ▤